"ROOM SERVICE,"
THE WOMAN CALLED

Colt in hand, Slocum cautiously padded barefoot to the door. He stood to one side, in case someone fired a shot through the thin door—stood there stark naked too, since the person on the other side had interrupted him while he was cleaning his clothes.

"I haven't ordered anything," he called out.

"I have."

This time he recognized the voice of Meg McGee, the gambler's lady friend. Slocum opened the door a few inches. "I ain't dressed."

Meg merely smiled and said, "You don't have to be."

JAKE LOGAN
SLOCUM'S GAMBLE

PLAYBOY
PAPERBACKS

Published simultaneously in the United States and Canada by Playboy Paperbacks, New York, New York. Printed in the United States
of America. Library of Congress Catalog Card Number: 81-84139.
First edition.

Books are available at quantity discounts for promotional and indus-
trial use. For further information, write to Premium Sales, Playboy
Paperbacks, 1633 Broadway, New York, New York 10019.

ISBN: 0-867-21015-X

First printing March 1982.

1

There were a fair number of things John Slocum had learned in the years since the war, chief among them how to stay alive. And one of the minor but important points leading to that most desirable end was that one simply does not, under any normal circumstances, choose to walk unannounced into another man's troubles.

But that was during the normal course of events —assuming there is or can be any normalcy in the life of a man like Slocum—and this morning Slocum was feeling anything but normal. He was, in fact, pissed. Thoroughly. With life. With the world in general. With Marlene Brooke in particular.

Marlene. Her name rang—sang, really—repeatedly through his thoughts and his emotions. Damn her. Bless her. No, damn her. That was better. But . . .

He shook his head. It did no good; it would have been impossible to drive the textures and the tastes of her out of his memory. He was not at all even sure that he wanted to.

Six months they had had together, one long, languorous, featherbed winter of her. And now the damn woman had disappeared. With scarcely a word of good-bye. With not a word of explanation. Damn her all to hell and gone anyhow.

Except Slocum did not really believe that, feel that way about her either. He would have if he could but . . . he just couldn't.

He sighed and slumped in his saddle, allowing the horse to pick its own pace and path along the now well-traveled stage route to Deadwood and the Black Hills.

He hadn't felt this utterly miserable about a woman since he was a kid, not since he was old enough to understand the deep and basic difference between having feelings for another human being and finding a place to dip one's wick.

Marlene Brooke. Christ, what a woman she was. Big and beautiful, elegant when clothed, and a raunchy, bawdy, drain-the-last-drop hoyden when she wasn't.

Six months. That was all they'd had; it had not been nearly enough. Stuck out there in the middle of the empty grass, just the two of them with a handful of seed stock, a little water, a lot of grass, and no other humans within forty miles to bother them. It was the closest John Slocum had come to having a home of his own, a woman to think of as his own for all the time to come, in . . . He could not remember how long. Did not *want* to remember how long it had been. Jesus!

And now . . . He shook his head again. He didn't understand it. The other day she had wakened as usual and rolled over in the deep featherbed he had come to think of as a haven set apart from the rest of the damned world, rolled over and began to nuzzle him as was her early morning habit, one long-fingered, carefully tended hand creeping lightly, teasingly, enticingly to his crotch as she wakened him and built his desire to match her own.

This too had become a habit with her over the months they had been together, this morning time of arousal and satiation. Before any thoughts of lighting the stove, before coffee or breakfast, always there was this to look forward to.

As he sometimes did, Slocum had pretended to cling to his sleep, allowing her the pleasure of waking him in her own hot and demanding fashion.

First the probing, caressing fingertips. And then the mouth. He groaned, just remembering her. The lips, seeking, pulling, bringing him practically to the brink before, finally, he was unable to contain himself any longer and began to move his hips in time with her efforts, driving himself deeper and deeper into her as she bent and worked to help him.

Then, on that morning, the abrupt, unexpected breaking of that physical union. She quit all contact with him, sat up in the bed beside him, and with a sweep of her arm threw the quilted coverlet back to expose them both to the briskly chill morning air.

She sat and stretched, arching her back and willing him to look at those magnificent breasts standing taut and firm and melon-sized above the sharp, inward dip of waist, above the full, womanly swell of her hips.

Slocum swallowed. He was getting a hard-on. Damn it.

He looked at her. It was what she wanted, and this was a woman he wanted to give to. There had been few enough of those in his life. None like this one. Not ever. He looked at her and felt a swelling obstruction rise in his throat at the marvelous sight of marvelous Marlene, and he . . . *cared* for her. He did not know any other word, or could not bring himself to use any other, to describe the feelings he felt for her then.

She smiled at him. He could remember that quite clearly. She had smiled and, lithe as a hunting cat, lifted herself onto her knees and straddled him as he lay on his back in the deep featherbed.

She opened herself to him and, with that haunting smile still on her lips, lowered herself onto the strong, hard pole that rose from his crotch.

He began to rise to meet her, but she lifted a finger to her lips to hold him silent and placed the fingertips of her other hand lightly on his chest to still his reflexive movements. Not once did she speak to him then, not once during the entire, sweet, warm encounter.

She silenced and stilled him, and then, slowly at first but with mounting intensity, she drew him deep inside her, raising and lowering her hips, timing herself to his rising sensations as if she possessed some form of entry into his thoughts and his feelings. Slowly at first and then faster, she pumped her beautiful hips up and down, straining against the size and the length of him, her own passions reflecting on her lovely face as she spiraled upward to join him.

At the end, too soon in coming, she was moaning aloud between clenched teeth, her lips drawn back in a grimace of passion that was no longer a smile, although it resembled one.

They exploded at the same instant, she driving herself down against him and he, unable to stop himself, lunging upward in a near-agony of pleasure from the white-hot intensity of his climax.

The bed frame shook and rattled unheeded on the earthen floor of the cabin that had been their home throughout the winter, and Slocum cried out in the early morning silence.

The woman had smiled again, a true and gentle smile this time, and allowed herself to collapse against the hard, muscular planes of John Slocum's chest.

Her breathing was harsh and ragged, and it took her long moments to regain her composure. With the finger of one hand she gently toyed with the small, dark patches of nipple on Slocum's chest, and eventually she sighed and kissed him tenderly beneath the ear. She sat up and removed herself from his satiated hips, deliberately reaching between her ivory thighs to capture with her fingers the running juices he had deposited inside her and smoothing them into already perfect skin as she might have used a scented lotion. She sighed, but this time he thought he could hear a measure of . . . regret, he thought . . . in the tone of her sigh.

"It's springtime, my dearest, dearest, John," she had said. He could still hear the sound of it now, captured and locked within his memory. "It is springtime, and there is a thing that I have to do now, my dearest John."

"But . . ."

"No." She laid her fingers against his lips again, blocking whatever he might have said, turning away any chance for him to protest or argue or try to convince. "This is something that I must do. I want you to accept what I have to say. I want you never to question me about it, John. It is something that I must do, and I want you to accept my judgment on the matter. Promise me that. You *must* promise me that."

Mutely, uncertain of what was to come, but already with a sense of foreboding, John Slocum nodded his head in silent agreement with her demands.

Whatever those demands, those needs would be, this was a woman he had come to admire and to trust as well as to care for. She was all woman but fully in command of herself. This was no fluttery, hothouse flower to be protected against herself. This was a mature woman as intelligent and as capable as she was beautiful, and he had come to respect her as well as to care for her. He nodded his agreement, and the simple movement of head and neck became a promise and a pledge that he knew he could not renege on without destroying all they had built between them. From his own proud point of view if not from hers.

"Thank you," she had said simply. "I must leave here now. Today. The place is still mine. You are welcome to stay. For as long as you wish. You can use it as if it were your own. If you like," she hesitated, "consider it to be your own. Lord knows you've given me enough pleasure in this crude little house to deserve this or anything else I have to offer, though that is little enough, to be sure."

Slocum had opened his mouth and would have spoken, but again she quieted him. "No. Please. No questions. You promised me that, John, and I know you would not break your word to anyone— and to me least of all. So remain quiet." She smiled. "There is a word you and I have never used between us, John. You are—I think you already know this—you are my own one, true love, John Slocum. I would not leave you lightly, and I do not do so now. But leave I truly must. For reasons that are not of your choosing nor of mine. Accept that. Remember me as fondly as I shall always remember you. And . . . accept this promise, John Slocum. If I can, and I do not know if it will be possible, but if I can . . . arrange things, I will return to you. Here, if you remain. Wherever you may be, if you have gone from this rude place of peace and rest on the Dakota prairie. But accept from me this one promise, the only promise I have ever made you and the only one I am ever likely to make you, John, my love. If I can return to you, I shall. In the meantime"—she smiled—"I will care for you as deeply tomorrow as I do today. And I always shall."

She left him then and began to dress, not bothering with fire or coffee or any of her usual morning patterns, and when she dressed, it was not in one of the plain and durable housedresses she normally wore for their days of work and pleasure on the shabby little homestead ranch in the middle of the empty grass. This time, from a trunk he had never investigated, she took out a beautifully tailored, impeccably stylish gown suitable for the grandest lady to travel in, and with meticulous attention to makeup and jewelry dressed herself as if in preparation for an audience before royalty. When she was done, Slocum was scarcely able to breathe. He already knew she was magnificent. But this . . . He shook his head. This was elegance beyond his wildest imaginings. He was in awe of the gracious spectacle now before him, and he could scarcely believe that he had romped and rutted and shared the sweat of heated passions with a woman of such stature and beauty. In a manner of speaking, she had already left him then. She was no longer his.

She dressed and turned to look at him for a long moment, her face an elegant mask that he could not begin to read, her emotions hidden and perfectly under control, whatever they might have been.

Finally, slowly, she moved to him. She flowed rather than walked as any ordinary, mortal woman might have done. She reached his side and held the backs of her fingers to his lips, gently touching first his lips and then, as gently, the unshaven stubble of beard that darkened his high-boned cheeks.

She gave him no kiss. But suddenly he had expected none. Suddenly a gesture as plebeian as a kiss would have been grossly out of place from a creature of such unbearable, unattainable quality.

And then she was gone, wafting away into the morning light as if she had never been.

She packed nothing, took none of her few ragged, tattered possessions with her when she left.

He sat inside, alone in the tiny cabin, until he heard her depart in the plain, hard-used buckboard that had served them as a ranch vehicle, knowing without understanding how the knowledge had come to him that on this morning she would want no assistance from him in the mundane details of hitching and harnessing.

He sat there alone in the silence she had left behind her, and when she was gone, John Slocum was not an hour behind her in his own departure.

He took time to roll his bedding and drop his meagerly few belongings into the trail-worn saddlebags that had been his home, his only home, for so very long. He turned loose onto the grass the few head of saddle stock they had accumulated over the past months. The animals could fend for themselves on the prairie grasses. And if ever Slocum—or Marlene—should return, the stock might still be grazing in the vicinity. If not . . . it really did not matter. Not to Slocum. Not, apparently, to the woman, either.

It took him little time to do these few things, and then he shut the door behind him for what might not prove to be the last time, and he stepped onto the hard-muscled, barrel-chested, long-traveling bay horse he had chosen to ride away from this place.

Behind him he left the bed unmade and still smelling faintly of their last night and that final, ineffably sweet coupling together. He left the stove laid ready for the match, and a pot of water with coffee grounds fresh and unboiled on its flat, cold surface.

And he rode away. Confused and uncertain and with a sense of quiet longing buried deep inside him that could only be filled if Marlene might somehow, sometime return.

John Slocum did not look back at the empty homestead as he rode aimlessly westward toward whatever road he might first strike and whatever uncared-about things might transpire while he was apart from this woman who had gained such an unexpected hold on his thoughts and feelings.

For the first few miles, though, he had a curious desire to once again be a small barefoot boy in short pants. Because if he had been, he could perhaps have allowed himself the luxury of tears, which in a grown man would have been unseemly.

2

Now, moping along the stage road that ran from Cheyenne down in Wyoming Territory—where Slocum had spent many a wild night in the past but for which he had no taste now—up toward the raw gold camp that had blossomed at Deadwood in the midst of the dark-pine beauty that was the Black Hills, Slocum rode with his head full of thoughts of the past and little attention to the present. Otherwise, because of the wisdom gained through hard experience, the sounds along the trail before him would likely have caused him to turn around and make Cheyenne his destination and not Deadwood. After all, he had no pressing business in either place. One would have been quite as good as the other, so long as whiskey was being sold to help a man forget his troubles.

He was already deep into the hills. Anywhere else, in the vast expanses of the nation, they would have been termed mountains. But here, in comparison with the mighty majesty of the great chain of the Rockies to the west, they were offhandedly, and probably improperly, dubbed hills. The bay wandered along the twin ruts of the recently cut stage road deep in the gulches that cut between

the precipitous, rocky slopes of the hills themselves.

Slocum rounded a granite outcropping at the
side of one of the hills and found that the road
here led across a grassy meadow in the center of
which was a halted stagecoach. The coach was not
the fancy Concord of the major lines, not the heavy
and often ornate rig that could in the largest models
accommodate as many as twenty-one not necessarily comfortable passengers. It was a light stage
—possibly a converted military ambulance, with
seats enough for nine paying passengers—light
enough to negotiate the sometimes steep trails
of a newly developing land.

Something was odd, slightly wrong, about seeing
a coach stopped in the middle of an open meadow,
though, and the wrongness of the view began to
penetrate even to Slocum's preoccupied thoughts.
A broken axle? he wondered. Trouble with a
wheel? No, that wasn't . . .

Shee-it! Both wheelers were bellydown in their
harness, flat on the ground and almost dragging
the swing and lead teams with them. And from
off somewhere in the peaceful-looking meadow he
could now hear a high-pitched "Yip-yip-yip yee-
ee-ee-hah!"

Shee-it, indeed. That was the shrill yap of some
damned fighting buck Indian having himself a
good time while he tried to kill somebody. Slocum
had heard it before. Never had learned to particularly like it.

But there was no question about it now. From
the long grass between his bay and where the disabled stagecoach was halted, he could see the dark
hair and copper-toned shoulders of an Indian rise
briefly out of hiding into a split-second view. Dur-

ing that fraction of a second an arrow arced forward from the patch of grass toward the coach.

At the same time, though, there was a puff of smoke from one of the previously empty coach windows; a moment later Slocum could hear the dull, booming bark of a rifle.

The Indian—Slocum could not be sure from the glimpse he had had, but he assumed the warrior would be a Sioux up in this country—dropped back out of sight, but Slocum thought he had seen the brave's head snap backward just before he disappeared from view. And he thought there might have been a faint mist-spray of red in the air immediately above where the Indian was now lying.

Damned good shooting if so, Slocum thought. You gotta give a man credit who can beef an enemy with that little bit of time for his shooting. He hurriedly backed his horse away from the brief scene, back around toward the protection of the rock outcropping he had just passed.

Shee-it. He didn't *think* he had been seen. Not by the people still holding out inside the disabled stage, nor by the attacking Indians who seemed so intent on dispatching them. But he could not be sure. There was at least the possibility that some of the Indians—there had to be a fair-sized party of them or they would not have dared attack the stage—might have seen him. And if they had . . . well, he had no desire at all to be cut off on an empty road with a bunch of Sioux warriors sniffing on his trail and him with no knowledge of the terrain around him. Damn it all, he had been so preoccupied with his own thoughts he had not even been taking his usual precautions about paying close attention to the land through which he traveled. The road behind him was almost as foreign to him as the road ahead, and he had paid no attention whatsoever to the lay of the country off to the sides of the public road.

Stupid bastard, he upbraided himself. But if they saw you poking around all alone back there they'll be after you, with or without the scalps of those stage passengers to gain the admiration of all the horny little gals back home.

Come to think of it, if they didn't do so well against the passengers, which was likely, judging by the shooting he had seen so far, they might be all the madder and all the more intent on fetching home at least one white man's scalp. Most Indians aren't much for making long-term events of a fight. They fight as much for fun as anything else, usually, and when they get bored they tend to give it up and do something else for a while. But these Sioux might take a notion to stick with the trail if they left the stage and got after Slocum instead.

Besides, he understood that the Black Hills were holy ground to the Sioux. They were supposed to have a sacred mountain up in this country, not too awful far from Deadwood, and who knew how they would go about defending that.

Slocum shook his head in a sort of sympathy for the Sioux. Poor bastards, he thought. They just didn't seem to know that once gold was discovered in their Black Hills it wouldn't matter worth a pile of horseshit if this country was sacred to them or not. Once the first whisper of a gold strike got out, they had effectively lost their title to the land, and there wasn't a treaty ever written nor any that ever could be written that would change a bit of that. Once the whites got onto the smell of gold it was all over for the Indians. The poor bastards just didn't know that yet.

Until they did learn it, though, there might be

hell to pay for any white man who chose to ride
through this country, and right now that was John
Slocum. Put into this awkward position by his own
stupidity, it was true, but put into it nevertheless.

Slocum was no fucking knight in shining armor.
He wasn't idiot enough to go riding into somebody
else's fight with his guns out just because it was
the proper thing to do. Hell no. That was a move
for suckers, the kind who wouldn't live long
enough to learn any better. John Slocum had lived
quite long enough to learn when to fight and
when to bow out with a few mumbled words about
discretion. The thing was, the more he thought
about it the more he thought his best move might
be to join those sharpshooters at the coach, where
he would have numbers on his side, rather than
take a chance on having to fight off a whole bloody
war party all by his lonesome.

So it was not generous valor but honest self-
interest that led Slocum to take his fully loaded
and ready Winchester into his left hand and palm
his always ready Colt in his right. And, when he
was as ready as he could hope to be, to spur the
bay hard around the curve in the road and thunder
down on the unsuspecting backs of those Sioux
braves parked in the grass of the meadow ahead.

"Eeeeeeaaaaahhhhh-*HHAHH!!!*"

Slocum's ululating rebel yell rang out in the
stillness of the afternoon, and he burst into the
open behind the Indians without warning.

He rode straight for the area where he had seen
the warrior before, and the sturdy bay's hooves
flashed like scythes as the horse charged forward.

Slocum saw a flicker of movement to his left,
and his Colt blasted a gaping hole in the breast-
bone of a painted young Sioux before Slocum had

time to rationally respond with the thought that this was an enemy in sight. His hands worked from ingrained reflex while his brain directed his knees to guide the racing bay.

An arrow swished and sizzled its way past his scalp from right to left, and Slocum's right hand responded automatically with the Colt. Another brave died with a soft lead bullet crushing the bridge of his nose and turning his black-and-yellow-stained features into a bubbling pink pulp of flesh and bone.

Another arrow flew by, farther from its intended mark this time, but it came from behind him. In seconds Slocum and the hard-charging bay had reached and passed the Indians' line of attack.

Slocum took no time to search for targets that were already behind him. He stretched low along the neck of the thundering horse and let out another rebel yell.

Ahead of him he could see the puffs of smoke from at least two guns as defenders in the stagecoach joined his fire, apparently hammering at targets Slocum had stirred up for them in the grass behind him.

The guns boomed loudly in the afternoon sunshine, and Slocum was up to them in scant seconds. He hauled down once on the bay's reins, sending the animal into a skidding, hock-down slide, and as soon as the horse's forward momentum was well broken, Slocum leaped off and hit the ground at a dead run. He reached the halted coach and catapulted himself into the air and through the nearest window as a cluster of arrows thunked into the wooden sides of the small coach around him.

*   *   *

"JasusMaryMotheruvGod!!!" someone squawled. "Will ye get yer fuckin' bony knees outta me handsome face now."

The inside of the small stagecoach was shadowed and almost dark in comparison with the bright sunlight outside. The air was close and still and smelled of sweat and whiskey and fear and gunsmoke. Somewhere over Slocum's head a carbine was bellowing, and under him someone else was sprawled in an awkward heap of arms and tangled legs and loud protests.

Slocum cautiously extricated himself from the jumble of twisted limbs and found that he had ended up lying atop a neatly dressed man who had bad breath, an aroused temper, and a Smith & Wesson revolver clutched firmly in the fingers of one large hand.

"Sorry," Slocum said with a grin. "I didn't mean to drop in on you unannounced like this."

"Quite all right," another man assured him. "You're more than welcome to join us, under the circumstances." That man, wearing a handsomely tailored black broadcloth suit and a yellow brocade waistcoat, was the one with the rifle. Even as he spoke, he shifted the gun for a snap aim toward the Indians, then grimaced and let it sag away from his still-watchful eye while he conversed with the new arrival.

"Speak for yourself, Mr. Lowe," the first man said. He regained a position on the seat-bench at the window Slocum had just entered and began to dust himself off. He straightened his tie but halted the motion long enough to throw a shot out the coach window. In the close confinement of the small vehicle the noise from the short-barreled gun was achingly loud. "As for me, I would've preferred a more civilized entry, sir, by way of the door there."

"Funny, I never thought of it at the time."

"You should have."

Slocum glanced around the cramped interior of the stopped vehicle. There were two other passengers in addition to the gentlemen with the firearms. Both of these seemed to be women, judging from the massive piles of petticoats in the spaces between the seats, but the owners of those garments were not up to formal introductions at the moment. Both were stretched out on the floorboards with what seemed to be every intention of burrowing through to reach the ground and, presumably, safety beyond.

Slocum tipped his hat toward the underclothes that greeted his view. "Ladies." One of the piles of lace stirred at least. The other did no more than continue to quiver.

"The ladies will join us later, sir," the man called Lowe said. His eyes remained focused outside the coach.

"Um. Yes." Slocum found the rifle he had dropped—or flung, to be more accurate—on the floor of the coach and poked it through the window toward the hidden Indians. "Been here long?" he asked politely.

"Long enough, I should say," Lowe said.

"Since morning," the other said.

"Long enough," Slocum agreed.

"I am Bertram Wilse," the man with the revolver said. He transferred the Smith to his left hand and, without looking toward Slocum, extended his right to shake.

"Pleased to meet you, Mr. Wilse," Slocum said. "And your friend here?"

"Lucius P. Lowe, at your service," Lowe answered for himself. "Luke to most of my friends and adversaries alike. And you, sir?"

"Slocum. John Slocum." Slocum regretted the admission almost as soon as it was made, but by then it was too late to recall. Damn, he thought to himself. The habits of concealment seemed to have deserted him during those long, pleasant months with Marlene. But the wanted posters that bore his name—and a few others he had used from time to time—would likely not have disappeared so easily.

The name brought Lowe's attention inside the coach for the first time since Slocum had made his crashing entry to the vehicle. "What a stroke of good fortune, Mr. Slocum. I am proud indeed to meet you, sir." The man extended his hand too.

"Actually," Slocum said, "I think we could use a bit of good fortune now. If all that wiggling I see in the grass out yonder is what I think it is, gentlemen, we are about to get kinda busy. Look sharp now, boys, here they . . . ."

3

". . . come." The inside of the stagecoach became a madhouse of sound as all three men opened up rapid-fire against the running, darting, dodging onslaught of Sioux warriors who popped suddenly from the tall grass. The Sioux raced forward a few erratic steps at a time and disappeared again as suddenly as they had come, only to reappear moments later and feet away for another rush toward the stagecoach defenders. But with each reappearance the Indians were steps closer to their goal.

There were more of them than Slocum had suspected. Perhaps they had been reinforced by new arrivals, he thought, because surely he had not made a dash through so damned many of them to get here. If he had been a man much given to second thoughts, he might very well have regretted his decision to join the men in the stagecoach when he might just possibly have gotten away undetected. But it was too late to be thinking about such things now. He had made the choice he thought best at the time. Now he could live—or die—with that judgment.

There must have been a score of the painted savages out there now, and with each new rush they were coming nearer. On the other hand, with each new rush there were fewer Sioux than there had been before. Slocum dropped two of them that he was sure of and might have dusted one or two besides. At Slocum's left shoulder, Bertram Wilse was making his ungainly Smith do some fancy talking in spite of its too-long grip and its hammer curl designed quite obviously with an orangutan's thumb reach in mind. To Slocum's right, Lowe was making a great deal of noise with his brass-bellied Henry rifle.

"There," Slocum called while he reloaded his Colt. He need not have bothered. No sooner was the brave in sight than Wilse's expert pistol shooting turned the fellow—beneath his paint he looked like he could not have been more than sixteen years of age—into a proverbial "good Indian."

"Nice shooting," Slocum said.

"Thanks."

"Any . . ." Slocum's Colt spat and another Sioux fell practically across the body of the one Wilse had just dropped. ". . . time."

The Indians came again, and once again the gunfire rolled like thunder out of the stagecoach windows. The warriors broke this time and ran, dropping down into the tallest of the grass at full retreat and wriggling away on their bellies as rapidly as they could crawl. The grass stems moved without wind in their wake.

Slocum breathed a bit easier. "Good work, boys. They seemed to be discouraged, at least for the time bein'. If we can keep this up we oughta be in good shape."

"We will," Lowe said hotly. His voice was shaking, but his resolve seemed very much intact, Slocum noted. The man was no great shakes with a gun, but there was nothing wrong with his nerve. Slocum had to give him credit for that.

Wilse coughed. "Per'aps you boys can do it alone, d'ye think?"

"What?"

Slocum turned to glance at Wilse. Shit. The man grinned at him, but Wilse's face was pale and strained and there was a trickle of blood showing at the corners of his mouth.

"I seem to've been tapped, you know."

"Bad?"

"Bad enough." He pointed down with his chin. At least one of the savages seemed to have a gun and to know how to use it. A bullet had pierced the thin sidewall of the coach to lodge somewhere in the vicinity of Wilse's belt buckle. There was a slowly spreading dark stain on the front of his vest, and a gutshot like that was going to have him howling with agony before the night was out. If he lived that long. Slocum had seen it often enough before, and a gutshot was never pretty. At the very best it was a lousy way to die.

"Sorry," Slocum said. He meant it.

Wilse grinned at him again. "You think *you're* sorry, bucko, you should know how sorry *I'm* being."

"I'll bet," Slocum said drily.

"Can you still shoot?" Lowe asked.

Slocum bobbed his head toward Wilse. "Our late companion here seems to've been shot."

"Late, did you say?"

"He damn well did," Wilse injected. "The red bastards've killed me, I reckon."

"Can you still shoot?" Lowe asked.

"Only if they come right quick again."

"He's in shock," Slocum explained. "When that wears off, in another few minutes, he'll be in a helluva shape."

"Do me a favor, boys?"

"Name it," Lowe offered magnanimously.

"Don't be so quick to pop your answer," Slocum said. "Not if he's about to ask the same thing I'd ask under the same circumstances. You might not want to hold good to your word on it."

"You got it, Mr. Slocum," Wilse said. To Lowe he added, "What the gentleman an' me understands, Mr. Lowe, is that a man in my, uh, delicate condition, he can't be helped except for one way. I'd rightly 'preciate it if one of you would be kind enough to do me the favor."

Slocum sighed. "I hate to see it, Mr. Wilse. You're a hell of a fine shot, you know."

Wilse smiled. "An' well I ought to be, boys. I'm a drummer by trade, but it's fine revolvers that I peddle. A demo man, from time to time, y'see. I'll leave my case o' goods to the one of you that does me the favor."

"That sounds fair," Slocum said.

"What the *hell* are you two people talking about?" Lowe demanded.

Slocum looked at him as if the man were a trifle dense. "He wants one of us to kill him."

"Gawd!"

"No, one of *us*. God'll get his chance at Wilse soon enough, though."

Lowe looked disgusted and turned his attention back toward the grass where the Indians presumably still lay in wait.

"Reckon that narrows the field, Wilse," Slocum drawled. "You want a good cigar or somethin' before you go?"

"No thanks. I never took up the habit."

Slocum nodded. "It is bad for your health, I've heard tell."

"Exactly." Wilse looked like he was going to say something more, probably something flippant and brave to show that he was not afraid of the hand the fates had dealt him. But a sudden flow of pain racked his features and twisted his already pale, drawn face into a death mask. "Ohhhhh, Christ-a-mighty."

Slocum nodded sympathetically. "Go easy, friend. You're too good a man to go screaming and clawing at your own guts." Slocum reached out to touch Wilse's suddenly sweating head, to soothe and calm the man. Slocum gently rubbed his temples and the back of his neck, and strong, hard fingers accustomed to the tasks of killing reached around Wilse's straining neck to find the pulsing cords of the artery lodged at the side of that neck. "Easy now, friend."

"Thanks," Wilse croaked hoarsely.

"You'd do as much for me."

"Aye."

Wilse grew quiet then, and after several moments Lowe looked at Slocum, then at Wilse. "The pain seems to have passed for the moment," he observed. "Poor bastard's slipped into a coma, I'd say."

"Something like that," Slocum agreed.

"Are you really going to do it? Kill him, I mean?"

"Did you want to?"

"Good Lord, no. I couldn't."

Slocum gave him a brief, disbelieving look but said nothing. Lowe wasn't much with a long gun, but unless Slocum's eyes had suddenly gone bad on him, that was a hideout gun tucked under Lowe's coat, and there was another suspicious bulge inside his right sleeve immediately above the cuff. Anybody who carried that many weapons concealed that carefully on his person was a man who expected to use them. And probably had. No,

Slocum thought, Luke Lowe was not likely to be as squeamish across a gambling table, say, as he made himself out to be here and now. But it hardly seemed the time to call the man on that subject. Not with maybe a dozen fighting Sioux still out there crawling around in the dust with the collection of fresh scalps on their minds and mayhem in their hearts.

"Pay attention now, Luke. I have a feeling they aren't done with us yet."

"You do the same, John, and we'll get out of this yet."

"You're an optimist, Mr. Lowe. I reckon I have to admire that."

"And you are the better shot, Mr. Slocum. So see to it, please, that you don't get yourself hurt." Lowe grinned. "I have faith in you, you see. And a feeling that my luck turned for the better when you rushed in here to join us."

"Then I hope you're a prophet as well as an optimist, because I think we could do with a bit of good luck from here on out."

They settled down at the windows to watch and wait for the next anticipated rush.

4

The loud, almost constant din of rolling gunfire had Slocum's ears ringing. The interior of the coach seemed to trap the noise and send it roaring back on the men, but it must have been even worse for the two women who continued to lie on the floorboards with their heads buried under protective arms. At least Slocum and Lowe could see and know what was going on outside the coach. The women would just be in terrified mystery with only the sounds to tell them that the men continued to resist.

Slocum shook his head and popped his jaw in an effort to clear his ringing ears, but it did no good. He sighed. Probably those women were better off not knowing how close the Sioux had come this time. Damn but they had been close! Within a few yards before finally they broke and ran for cover. Oddly enough, they persisted in making their charges from only one direction, though. That was fortunate. Slocum doubted that he and the poor-shooting Lowe could have held the coach against an assault from all sides.

He craned his neck and tried to peer toward the front of the vehicle. At least the Sioux had not yet been able to reach the four horses that remained alive in the hitch. The two dead wheelers still lay where they had dropped, and the other four stood, no doubt uncomfortably, in their harness. It was probably the horses as much as the scalps that the Indians wanted, Slocum thought. Otherwise the remaining stout-bodied animals would long since have been slain.

"Where's your driver and guard?" Slocum asked unnecessarily. He expected he already knew the answer.

"Dead," Lowe said.

Slocum was not amazed. He would have been surprised by any other answer.

"They both went down in the first volley of arrows," Lowe said. "Never got a shot off, either one of them, I don't believe. The horses went down next. We've been here ever since."

Slocum nodded. "At least if we do get out of this we'll have transportation."

"Yeah." Lowe did not sound like he was overjoyed by their prospects for survival.

It was getting on toward dusk now, and the light in the meadow was beginning to fade. Slocum was not carrying a watch, but he did not think it was all that late, even though a man tends to lose track of time in a fight. He thought it more likely that the high walls of rock and dense pine growth made twilight a relatively early occurrence here at all times.

"Something—" Slocum did not have time to finish the sentence. An arrow sped from a clump of grass. Slocum's snapped pistol shot followed immediately behind the glimpse of motion, and he thought he saw another Sioux warrior flop briefly into view with a convulsion of pain before the grass again hid the target from sight.

"He didn't come anywhere close that time," Lowe said optimistically.

"I wouldn't be so sure," Slocum told him.

The coach rocked slightly on its springs of leather strapping as ahead of them one of the draft horses began to squeal and snort.

"Reckon he found his target," Slocum said. The wounded horse was rearing and pawing now, but the disturbance lasted only for a matter of moments before they could hear the dull thud of an immensely heavy body striking the earth. The movement of the coach stopped again.

"Shit," Lowe moaned.

"It might be a good sign," Slocum said. "If they're killing the horses now, it might mean that they've given up on the notion of taking them. An' that might mean that they're fixing to pull out of here."

"I hope you're right."

It was definitely darker now than it had been just a few minutes earlier. Another arrow swished through the air without Slocum having any chance to see where it had come from. And another horse began to scream in pain.

"Look sharp now," Slocum warned.

But there was little need for the advice. Again and again the flights of arrows found their marks, and soon there was no more motion or sound from the six-up of harnessed, dead horses.

"Shee-it," Slocum mumbled.

Together he and Lowe crouched within the embattled coach with their guns ready, waiting for an assault to spring up from the growing darkness. But there was nothing more to be seen or heard in the dim, gray light beyond the darkened coach interior.

Slocum thought he could make out the faint

sounds of hoofbeats on rock far away. He sat upright for the first time in several hours. "I think
they've gone," he said.

"Are you sure?"

"Who's sure? I said I *think* they have. You don't
get no guarantees on that score, neighbor. Not
from those Sioux, you don't. They could be a mile
away from here right now, or, dark as it is, half a
dozen of them could be layin' six feet from the
wheels of this here wagon ready to jump the first
one of us that shows himself."

Lowe chewed his lower lip. He looked more
nervous now than he had during the last attack.
"What are we going to do about it?"

Slocum shrugged. "Go take a look, I reckon."
He sighed. It was, after all, his idea. "You set there
where you are. Wait a minute, you got anything
but that rifle?"

Lowe shook his head.

"Hold onto this, then." Slocum handed him the
Smith & Wesson revolver Wilse had been shooting.

"Thanks." Lowe peered around Slocum's broad
shoulders toward the dead salesman. "I guess he
slipped off sometime during the fight, huh?"

"Something like that," Slocum said. "Sit where
you are, Lowe, and keep your ears open. A man
can't depend on his eyes for fighting in the dark.
Use your ears. If they happen to be out there an'
they just happen to kill me, you do what you think
best, but was I you I think I'd kill these two ladies
here before I did anything else."

Lowe nodded. It was almost too dark now for
Slocum to see the movement of his head. There
was no reaction at all from the women, although
it would have been impossible for them not to
have heard what Slocum was saying. Neither of
them even seemed to quiver any more than they

had been doing right along. Poor, miserable cows, Slocum thought. Maybe they just didn't *want* to understand. They must be a pair of real losers.

There was neither any time nor any point in worrying about them now, though. Slocum's immediate thoughts had to be for the safety of his own head of hair. If that was gone, he really could not care less what happened to theirs. He checked to make sure his Colt was fully loaded and slid out through the door opposite where the Indians had been lying in wait during the day.

It felt very good to stand upright again after so many hours inside the confinement of the small stagecoach, and Slocum stood for a moment to stretch and enjoy the clean, fresh, crisply chill evening air.

He was not wasting time, though. Instead he was listening. He had not given good advice to Luke Lowe just to ignore it himself. At night a man's best line of defense is his sense of hearing. As far as Slocum could determine, and his hearing was quite good indeed, there was nothing moving anywhere near the coach or, for that matter, the entire meadow.

Which told him very little. If there were Sioux lying in ambush in the grass near the coach, they would not be moving now. They would be waiting for him to show himself.

All right, boys, he silently told them, we'll give you some bait. Let's see if you're quick enough to take it before I take you.

With deliberately heavy footsteps John Slocum stepped around the back end of the stagecoach, his active, and edgy, brain filtering out the sounds of his own movement while trying to tune in on any noises that might be made by someone else.

Behind him Lowe or perhaps one of the women

coughed. Slocum damn near shot whoever it was before he realized it was one of his own party.

Jesus. He stopped and took a deep breath before he moved again.

In ever widening circles he cat-footed through the tall grass away from the coach, but all he raised was an occasional flutter of grasshoppers or other insects disturbed by his passage. As far as he could determine, the meadow was empty except for himself and the remaining passengers from the useless coach.

"Come on out," he called. "It's time for us to get out of here while we can."

Slowly, disbelievingly, Lowe and the two women emerged. It was too dark in the moonless night for Slocum to see their faces, but he knew their expressions would be a mixture of relief and apprehension.

"Are you sure . . . ?" It was a woman's voice. Soft and nervous. She sounded young, but you can't tell anything from a woman's voice. He had known ancient battle-axes that sounded like teenage girls. And once or twice he had encountered some that were just the other way around. The two women were no more to him now than a pale blur against the darkness.

"Nobody's sure, lady," Slocum said. "But they sure seem to've cleared out. We better get out of here while we can."

"Shouldn't we wait . . . ?" It was the same woman again.

"For what? The cavalry? They ain't coming, lady. Nobody knows we're here 'cept the Indians. They're the only ones likely to come looking for us. An' we don't hardly want to be here if they do try again in the morning. No, we gotta get out of here. Now."

Lowe walked forward along the line of dead horses, but if he was hoping to find one still in condition to pull the coach he was doomed to disappointment. Even Slocum's bay seemed to have run off or, more likely, to have been picked up and taken along by the Sioux warriors as their only trophy of the fight.

"What about all our things?" the other woman asked. She sounded much older than the first who had spoken. Perhaps it was a mother-daughter pair traveling together, Slocum speculated.

"Leave them. The Sioux will likely paw through it all come daylight. Whatever they don't want someone else can fetch into Deadwood for you another time. Right now we got no way to carry anything except ourselves."

With a sigh of regret, Slocum realized the truth of his own words. Damn it. Wilse had given him a perfectly good salesman's case filled with fancy handguns and ammunition, no doubt, but Slocum did not have time now to even examine the contents of the case, much less carry it with him. It would be foolish to take the time to try to find it in the dark amid all the luggage and freight strapped to the roof and on the carry-platform at the rear of the light coach. Damn it!

And worse yet, the bay, wherever it was, had been carrying virtually everything Slocum owned, including nearly all of his money. That had been in his saddlebags. He felt in his pockets. He had perhaps $10, ten or fifteen rounds of ammunition, and a pocketknife to his name.

He grinned into the night, and if the others could have seen that grin they might well have been frightened by it. John Slocum had been in worse shape before, and if he lived he likely would be again. At least this time he had a good Colt on his hip and a Winchester repeating rifle in his hands. He wasn't so bad off after all.

"Come on, people. Let's get to walking before we have us some visitors."

With a grumble of complaints both male and female behind him, Slocum began to leg it up the road toward Deadwood.

5

Slocum woke up in a foul humor. They hadn't made five miles distance from the disabled stagecoach the night before until the women's bitching made them quit the hike and look for a place off the road where they could get some sleep. Alone, Slocum could have gone five times that far or more before daylight—and he certainly had considered going on alone—but with the women to drag them down . . . He still was unhappy about it, but a man simply doesn't turn white women loose to fend for themselves when there are a bunch of playful Sioux on the prod looking for scalps. And Slocum did not think Lowe would be of much use if it came to a fight in the open. The man had already proven himself pretty well useless with a gun at any distance greater than that across a gambling table. For all Slocum knew, in spite of those hideout guns Slocum had spotted, Lowe might be useless there too. Damn. What a crowd to be saddled with.

He sat up and looked around. The first pinkish yellow rays of morning sun were streaming over the nearest abrupt hill to the east of them, and it was only the deep shadow at the base of the hill that had let Slocum sleep as long as he had. As it

was, he had chosen to bed down slightly apart
from the rest of them. Let Lowe sleep where the
women might think he could protect them. Hell,
maybe he had come to know and like them on the
trip before the Sioux hit. If so, the man was more
than welcome to them. In the mood Slocum was in
right then, he was willing to consign all women—
well, nearly all—to perdition or worse. Fuck them
all.

No, he thought, retract that. Right now he didn't
even feel like *that*. At least a gun and a horse
wouldn't bitch at a man until they wore him out.

He rubbed the back of his neck and ran a none
too clean hand over his unshaven cheeks. Even his
razor had disappeared with the bay horse. Shit.
His mood was getting worse and worse the longer
he sat there.

So he stood and looked around.

There was nothing he could spot along the road
that lay below them nor anywhere else in sight.
If the Indians were trailing, they were doing a
good job of staying out of sight. Or just hadn't
gotten this far yet. There was no way to tell; they
would just have to wait and see.

Satisfied that no one was about to jump the
small, footsore party, Slocum brought his attention
back to their own crude camp, which consisted
simply of all of them finding a reasonably soft
patch of slanted earth on the hillside and lying
down to sleep.

Son of a bitch, Slocum told himself.

If he had known *this* was what he was grousing
at the night before he would have . . . Who knew
what he might have done. The woman lying over
there, still asleep, her limbs open and vulnerable,
her features soft and innocently angelic in repose,
was . . . beautiful.

Slocum took a deep breath. Gawdalmighty! Beautiful. A highly overused word, Slocum thought. Including by one J. Slocum himself. But in this case . . . it just wasn't enough to describe the beautiful, incredible creature who was lying there in silent sleep.

Her face might have been sculpted by an old-school French artist working from one of those elegant miniature paintings like they hung in the fanciest of galleries. Or from a delicate, perfect cameo.

Cheekbones slightly high, with the hollowed, satin perfection of the flesh beneath molded softly toward a smallish chin that gave her face a lovely heart shape. Lips full and moist even in sleep. Nose a delicate carving in alabaster, slightly pointy and tip-tilted. Eyelashes dark and curling above the softness of the ivory pads leading from nose to cheeks. Hair smooth jet, as sleekly black as a raven's wing, so dark the highlights imposed by the rising sun seemed almost blue. Eyes a deep, intense shade of violet, unlike anything Slocum had ever seen in his years of admiring beauty in woman and beast alike.

Eyes . . . ! They were open. He had been caught staring at her.

Unconsciously Slocum recoiled, stood swiftly above her to his full, lean, muscular height. He had without thought felt himself drawn to her side. Now she had found him out in his uncouth action, and for a brief moment he felt as embarrassed and abashed as a schoolboy caught placing a frog into teacher's desk drawer.

He stood towering over her still-supine body— he groaned, he did not want to think about her body, tiny-waisted, full-bosomed, long and slim as

she lay on her impromptu bed of crushed grasses
—and willed himself not to redden.

The woman stretched, slowly and with an obvious awareness of what the motion did to the taut-
ness of the fabric of her gown pressing against the
superior force of large, firm breasts. She gave him
a catlike smile. The pink, quivering tip of her
tongue rolled languorously, deliberately across her
lips and left them wetter and softer-seeming than
before.

"Yes?" she asked. The one, simple word was
uttered in a voice that was throaty with invitation.
It was a voice he did not recognize from the complaining tones of the night before. It was a voice
which in that one word could convey volumes of
unspoken meaning.

Slocum stiffened—his shoulders, his cock was
already long-since erect from the sight of this
woman—and reacted with gruffness in his lingering embarrassment.

"Time to get under way again. Them Sioux
could still be trailing us. Get up." The last words
were spoken harshly, as a command.

The woman smiled. She seemed to understand
all too well the reason for the sharp tone of voice.
Her eyes fell slowly and deliberately from Slocum's
face to the impressive bulge that threatened to
burst through the buttons of his jeans. "Whatever
you say." She came to her feet in a lithe, flowing
motion, and Slocum discovered that she was fully
a head shorter than he, but her vitality and her
beauty made her seem much taller and even fuller
of figure than she actually was.

He found it difficult to breathe with her standing
so near his chest that her magnificent breasts were
nearly brushing his shirt buttons. He took a half

step backward to give himself room. "Wake the others," he ordered brusquely.

"As you wish."

She turned away, and the awesome hold she had over his senses dissipated. For the first time in several minutes, Slocum was able to concentrate once again on the dangerous business of survival.

Slocum gulped for air. It was a damned good thing, Slocum thought, that the Sioux had not chosen that moment to attack their makeshift camp. Right then he suspected they could have taken his hair to decorate their lodgepoles and he would have given the bastards a silly smile while they sharpened their knives to do the job.

Gawd but that was a whole bunch of woman.

6

They reached Deadwood mid-morning of the following day. It would have been an even longer walk with the women to slow their progress, but another of the unscheduled, haphazardly run stagecoaches into the still-rough mining camp had come along and given them a ride the last ten miles of the journey.

Slocum and the beauty who called herself Meg McGee—a classical Black Irish beauty—had fared well enough under the demanding pace Slocum had set for them. Lowe had been limping a little in his decorative but impractical shoes, their spats long since discarded as a nuisance. It was the other woman, a plain, mousy, quiet little thing named Jennifer Porter, who had held them back the most.

Meg, as Slocum had quickly come to think of her, had shown a game spirit after that first confused night of flight from the Indians.

The arrival of the war-party survivors created a flurry of excitement among the miners who occupied this desolate, ugly, earth-brown blotch on the natural beauty of the Black Hills, and for half an hour or so there was loud talk about mounting a party of armed men to search out and punish the offending Sioux, but the talk was inspired by whiskey and hot blood and inevitably cooled once the speakers realized that in order to conduct such a chase they would have to be away from their claims, leaving their gravel-walled glory holes open to the possibility of claim jumping. After all, a white man's revenge against a red Indian was all very well and good. But it could not interfere with the flow of commerce or the chance of achieving the riches they had all come here to find.

Finally the excitement ebbed, and the newcomers were directed toward one of the establishments that passed as a hotel in Deadwood.

Slocum trailed along behind Meg and Lowe toward the hotel, while the almost unnoticeable little Jennifer left the group without a backward glance and took off in her own direction, apparently having a destination in mind other than the hotel.

Good riddance, Slocum thought. He had not liked Miss Porter all that much. Particularly in comparison with the incomparable Meg.

As for Slocum, he was going with the others simply because he wanted to know which room Meg McGee would be inhabiting in this ugly camp.

As they walked, he looked around for the first time. He was neither surprised nor disappointed by what he saw, but he was depressed nonetheless. Damn but Deadwood was a miserable place! Probably, judging from the country they had been passing through ever since they entered the Black Hills 'way back where, this too must recently have been a tree-shaded, green, and lovely little gulch set amid the surrounding natural beauty and indistinguishable from it.

But once the bright and gleaming color of gold had shown itself in the gravel of this particular gulch, the place had changed—and not for the better. Now the sudden influx of miners had made it an altogether different place from what it must have been less than two years before.

The claims had been staked as rapidly as the men flooded into the raw, new camp, and as soon as they were staked they were stripped of every scrap of vegetation. Deep holes, each a hoped-for glory hole, had been gouged into the gravel subsoil, and each needed to be shored with timber. The famed pines that gave the Black Hills their name were quickly used up, and the eager miners spread out around the camp of Deadwood in search of more timber for their underground burrowings. They left behind them bare earth and barren rock, which must have been an impossible quagmire in the rainy season, Slocum thought. From the town itself he could now see nothing that grew, not even grass. The grasses had been trampled underfoot by the passage of thousands of heavy boots and disappeared as surely as the trees had before them. Now the entire gulch was a study in drabness, with only a few painted signs and—seen on an occasional balcony or through an open window— gaudy petticoats to give the place any color at all.

A man could damned near forget what colors were if he stayed very long in Deadwood, Slocum thought.

He sighed. But he sure had no choice about staying. One way or another he had to make himself a stake, if only to get the hell out of here. Everything he owned, with the exception of his guns and his Bowie, had disappeared on that damned bay horse when the Sioux got into the act back there. He had no way out of Deadwood unless he wanted to hoof it back the way he had come. And considering how far it was down to Cheyenne or up toward Bozeman, that was not an attractive proposition.

He felt in his pockets. He had been carrying practically nothing on his person. Everything had been in those saddlebags. He could afford a room and maybe some meals. But he doubted the $10 would last very long.

Shit. Until he realized that, he had been feeling pretty good just because he had gotten here alive. Now he wasn't so bloody delighted with the way things had turned out. Still, he trudged along behind Lowe and Meg and followed them into the crude hotel that was supposed to be Deadwood's finest.

Lowe glanced behind him and saw Slocum walking in the same direction. Since the attack, all of them, including Lowe, had been fairly quiet, a little distant from one another. There certainly had been no camaraderie built up among them as a result of the plight they had found themselves mutually drawn into.

"Will you be taking a room here too, John?" he asked, slowing his pace so they were walking side by side. Meg slowed too and walked with them, Slocum noted.

And Lowe unconsciously took Meg's elbow to guide her along with them. Interesting. Damned interesting, Slocum thought. They had not seemed particularly close while the threat of another Indian attack lay over them. Then it had pretty much been everyone for him or her own self. Now Lowe seemed to be assuming control of things for himself and for Meg as well.

"I doubt it," Slocum said. "The place looks a bit high-toned for what I got left in my jeans. My stake was on that damned horse."

Lowe smiled. It seemed a curious reaction to such a piece of information. "Perhaps you would care to join us for dinner, then. As my guest?"

Slocum shrugged. "Why not?" Hell, he wasn't going to turn down a good feed. Not with his pockets so near to empty. If he was lucky he could find a poker table—half the wood that had been used to construct this camp probably went into the making of poker tables, if he could judge by the other mining holes he had seen in the past—and maybe improve his fortunes before dark.

But it had been several days since his last chowdown, and he sure as hell was hungry. That took precedence over the poker right now.

"Good. I have a proposition you might want to consider, John," Lowe said.

"If you don't mind, Luke, it, uh, might be a good idea if you was to forget what name I was traveling under on the road back there. Admissions in a moment of stress shouldn't oughta be held against a man, if you know what I mean."

Lowe smiled brightly. "Indeed I do," he said. Now that they were back in a town, back where he seemed comfortable in a familiar environment, Luke Lowe seemed an altogether different and more commanding man than he had back there on the dusty road with the threat of another Sioux attack hanging over them at any and every moment. "Do you have a preference? I mean, I have heard of you. And while I don't know of any particular interest in your whereabouts up here, well . . ." He let the obvious go unsaid. There were wanted posters out on John Slocum in too many parts of the country for him to feel particularly secure anywhere at this point.

Slocum grinned. "If the subject comes up, Luke, I'm John Wilse." The name was conveniently in his mind. And he had liked, however briefly, the name's original owner.

"Fair enough. You got that, Meg?"

The woman nodded. She, too, seemed quite different now that they were in Deadwood. On the road she had seemed more in charge of herself than she did here. Here she seemed smaller, somehow. Shrunken. An extension of Lowe's will rather than a beautiful woman in command of herself and of the men who were near her.

Curiouser and curiouser, Slocum thought. But apparently Lowe's instructions to her would not be questioned, and as far as Meg McGee was concerned he was now John Wilse.

Slocum wondered if he should look up the mousy little Miss Porter and mention the new name to her as well. Or if that would just create problems rather than solve them. He decided it would more likely cause problems than otherwise. He had no real idea what the Porter woman did, but in his own imagination he had pegged her as a hatmaker or dressmaker or some such drab little business that a spinster lady was apt to get herself into. A woman like that would never have heard of John Slocum. Drawing attention to himself with her would be like throwing coal oil into a wood stove. Stupid.

"I'll give you fair warning, Luke," Slocum said. "Right now I could eat an ox an' not leave enough neckbones to make a good broth."

Lowe smiled. "I've noticed a pinch of hunger in the gut, myself, John Wilse. But I think I have ample funds to take care of our needs."

"Good."

They reached the hotel, and Lowe took a moment to check into a room, demanding the key to the largest, finest appointed suite available—which Slocum doubted would be much in a place like this anyway—before he headed for the dining room.

Slocum also noticed that Meg McGee made no

mention of a room for herself. Apparently she was
expected to share Lowe's. Damn, Slocum thought.
And he had really been looking forward to a romp
on top of that beautiful body, too.

It took no time at all to order their meal. The
place had little to offer. Beef, beans, and biscuits
or go somewhere else. Lowe told the waiter to keep
bringing it until they hollered uncle. And to fetch
a gallon or two of coffee to start them off right.

The food was on the table within moments, and
for quite a long time there was no conversation
possible as the three of them gave their attention
to satisfying a need that had been too long building. Finally Lowe leaned back with a satisfied
belch and signaled the waiter. "Two cigars if you
please, my good man. And would you have someone show the lady to my room."

"Yessir." The man—he did not look like a waiter
and probably was a would-be miner who had gone
bust on a lousy claim—bowed away from the table.
Meg, accepting her obvious cue, excused herself
and disappeared.

Lowe turned his head briefly to watch Meg's
well-rounded rump. "A fine, healthy animal," he
murmured. "And the only kind of livestock a
gambling man should own." He grinned.

Slocum grunted noncommittally. Lowe obviously was staking his own kind of claim, however
crudely. With very little effort, Slocum thought, he
could develop a fairly hearty dislike for Luke Lowe.

When his attention returned to Slocum, Lowe
was all business. "Tell me Mr., uh, Wilse," Lowe
said, "have you any particular plans here? Forgive
me, but you do not have the appearance of a man
who can be deluded into believing that a grubby
hole in the ground is going to make him suddenly
wealthy. Even if decent claims were still available.

Nor does your reputation lend itself to that likelihood."

"I expect you have a reason for asking?" Slocum's voice was dangerously taut now. Personal questions were something a man did not ask in this part of the country. He wondered briefly if Lowe was looking for trouble now, although he could think of no reason for the man to do so. Unless he thought he could capitalize on some of the reward fliers that might still be in effect with John Slocum's name on them.

"I do not, I assure you," Lowe said quickly. He must have heard the change in Slocum's voice, probably understood the imminent danger he was in. "I mean, that is, that I do have a reason for asking. But not one that would, uh, be a disadvantage to you, sir. I assure you."

No, Slocum thought, the man was too flustered now to have been thinking anything like that. And, he remembered, too poor a shot as well. That was a handicap no one was going to accuse John Slocum of, and Lowe obviously knew it.

"My intentions," Lowe said quickly, "are to offer you a way out of your current, uh, situation."

Lowe had his hands carefully placed on top of the table, Slocum saw, curling around his coffee cup. He was taking no chances that Slocum might misinterpret and think he was going for that hideout pistol beneath his coat. Deliberately he rolled his right hand palm upward on the table. In that position Lowe could not easily bring the sleeve gun into play either. He smiled.

"I'm listening."

"Yes, well, as I hinted to you earlier, my, uh, financial position has been unimpaired by our recent difficulties. And as I have also indicated to you, Mr. Wilse, my livelihood derives from the gaming tables." His smile was somewhat oily now. "A town such as this one promises good fortune for me, my friend."

Slocum did not particularly like that reference to a friendship that did not in fact exist. Slocum picked his friends a hell of a lot more carefully than that.

"But," Lowe went on, "placer miners are notoriously, shall we say, unstable persons. Given to delusions and excitement. And you undoubtedly noticed early in our acquaintance, John, that I am not particularly, uh, adept with a firearm. I have certain talents and abilities, but that is not among them. What I propose, sir, is that you accept employment. On my behalf, as it were. To offer a certain, uh, protection. If you know what I mean."

Slocum nodded. A bodyguard was what Lowe wanted. Probably would have need of one, too. It isn't particularly safe to bilk a whiskey-soaked miner out of his earnings, even honestly. Slocum doubted that Luke Lowe was notorious for his honesty at the tables, either.

"I get your drift. You want somebody watching your backside. So what's your offer?"

In a way, Slocum hated to ask that last question. But judging from the high price that desk clerk had been asking for a single lousy room and from the prices he had already seen on the menu in this poor excuse for a hotel restaurant, Deadwood was not going to be a cheap place to live in. It could take a man a hell of a long time to get enough of a stake together to get out of this shithole. If Luke Lowe could give him a shortcut, he would have to consider it.

"Fifty dollars a week, Mr. Wilse," Lowe said without hesitation.

It was, Slocum admitted, a princely salary. A

dollar a day was a normal wage. Half that again for gun wages. A really top gunman, which Slocum did not particularly care to become in any event, and which was not likely to be paid in a dump like this anyway, would not likely get more than $15 per week. And $50? Shit, it seemed like an offer he couldn't hardly refuse. Which no doubt was exactly what Luke Lowe intended.

"Plus keep," Slocum said. He said it without emphasis, as he would have announced a raise at a poker table. He knew better than to step into a first offer.

"Done," Lowe said quickly. "Fifty a week plus keep. I'll arrange a room for you next to my own and you can sign for anything you want here at the hotel. I will, of course, expect you to refrain from participating in any of my games." He smiled. "For your own good and mine."

"In other words, you don't expect to lose," Slocum observed.

Lowe's smile became broader. "My dear sir, no gambler ever expects to lose. It is the nature of the game, is it not?"

"Whatever you say."

Lowe seemed quite pleased to hear those words come from John Slocum's mouth.

Lowe pushed himself away from the table. "There is just one other thing then, Mr., uh, Wilse."

"Yes?"

"I wouldn't like it if you were to, uh, rustle from my herd of livestock. If you know what I mean."

"I know what you mean," Slocum said. Lowe didn't want him screwing around with the delectable Meg.

Well, Slocum hadn't lied to Lowe. He *did* know what the man meant. On the other hand, Slocum hadn't actually made any promises in that regard, either. And if the lady happened to want to mix sweat with him sometime, he was not likely to turn her down. Not that one.

They left the table, Slocum feeling much better than he had an hour before, and went to arrange Slocum's room.

7

Slocum lay stretched full length and naked on the big, soft bed that was much nicer than he had expected to find in such a dump of a town. The hotel accommodations actually were not so bad. And the only way for him to get a room adjacent to Lowe's suite was for Lowe to get him one of the better rooms in the place. Not so bad at all, actually.

The gambler had told him to rest through the afternoon, that he himself was tired after their ordeal and intended to nap, that they probably would spend most if not all of the night at whatever gambling tables looked the best in this busy, gold-crazy camp. So Slocum had resigned himself to the chore of allowing another man to master his movements. At least for the time being. At least until he got a horse and a reasonable stake together. But the prospects of a dull afternoon in an empty hotel room were not to John Slocum's liking. He was not a man for sleeping when the sun was up, especially since the walk at the pace set by the two women had been anything but physically demanding, despite Luke Lowe's discomfort. But for the moment, all Slocum could do was rest in preparation for what might be a long night and wait for his employer to summon him to his new duties.

Slocum yawned and looked once again around him. The Colt had been cleaned, and his Winchester as well. His clothes were in as decent a condition as he was likely to get them without the assistance of a laundry. And he had no extras to wear while his lone outfit could be cleaned. He was, he decided, in a hell of a shape, everything considered. But that would end soon enough—as soon as Luke Lowe uncorked his wallet and paid Slocum a week's wages. He wondered if a measly $50 would be enough of a stake, then regretfully realized it would not. Not here in Deadwood, with a horse and ammunition to be purchased. Without those he could not even hope to pull off a robbery. And the boys around this town seemed pretty well on the prod looking for robbers anyway. Deadwood probably would not be the easiest place to pull a successful heist, which implies as well a successful escape afterward. The trails away from the town were just too limited to allow that. No, for the time being Slocum seemed to be stuck where he was. He yawned again.

A light tapping at his door roused him from the half sleep he had drifted into, and his hand flashed without time for conscious thought to the heavy Colt that hung on the bedpost beside him.

He was not dressed, having sponged off his dusty clothing earlier, so he padded barefoot to the door with the Colt held ready in his right hand.

"Who is it?" He was standing beside the door, not in front of it. If someone wanted to throw a shot through the thin partition it would turn out to be more dangerous for the attacker than the attacked that way.

He heard a low-voiced chuckle. "Room service." It was a woman's voice.

"I haven't ordered anything."

"I have." A bit louder this time. He recognized the voice as belonging to Meg McGee. Slocum opened the door a few inches.

"I ain't dressed."

"You don't have to be."

"Suit yourself then." He let the door swing the rest of the way open.

The woman stepped inside.

Since he had last seen her, down in the dining room, she had worked some feminine wonders. She was no longer wearing the tattered, dirty gown she had been hiking in. Now she had on a flowing, elegant creation that reminded him of something he had seen not too long ago. It came back to him then: Marlene. Jesus. He couldn't believe he had forgotten about her so completely, so soon. But Meg's gown definitely reminded him of the garment Marlene had taken from that trunk before she left.

Between the thoughts of Marlene and the appearance of Meg—even lovelier than before, with touches of rouge and powder on her beautiful face now—Slocum sprang to instant attention immediately below his waist. It had been too damned long since Slocum had had a woman. And this was a woman who would have inflamed him even if he had just come from a solid week in a whorehouse.

Meg's eyes dropped to the rock-hard pole that was jutting forward between them. Those beautiful violet eyes widened, and she wet her lips with the tip of her tongue. "My oh my," she said. "I've seen studhorses that weren't hung that well."

"Delicate little flower, ain't you," Slocum said.

"Not hardly." She laughed and crossed the room to perch on the side of his bed. "Why don't you close that door, John. And lock it."

"Why don't I do that little thing." He did.

"Poor Luke is all worn out from our walk," she said. "He's sound asleep now and no company at all. I was hoping you might be able to . . . amuse me."

"Amuse, huh? I never heard it called that before."

"It's as good a word as any other."

"I suppose so." He crossed the room and stood in front of her. His pulse, throbbing wildly in the long pole that was pointed at her chin, caused his cock to gently bob up and down. The movement seemed to fascinate her.

She reached out and with surprisingly gentle fingertips traced the length of him. She cupped his balls in the warmth of her palm and hefted them. "Nice," she said.

"A gentleman always likes to receive a compliment from a lady."

"But is it useful?" She licked her lips again.

"We could find out, I suppose."

"Yes. Perhaps we should."

Quickly, her attention admiringly fixed on Slocum's midsection, she began to unbutton the bodice of her gown. Within seconds she was as naked as he, and her body was all he might have expected. And more.

He had no idea how old she was. She might have been anywhere from twenty to thirty-five. But she had the body of a girl. A fully developed and marvelously endowed girl, but a girl nonetheless. Her breasts were large, but they were as firm as a fourteen-year-old's, and her skin was unblemished ivory for the full, voluptuous length of her. The beauty of her flesh was highlighted but not diminished by a jet black triangle of softly curling pubic hair.

"Fuck me," she said softly.

"In a minute." She already wanted him. Had wanted him to begin with or she would not have come here. Wanted him all the more after seeing the weight of meat that he carried between his thighs. He was not likely to lose her now, and he was determined that he was not going to let things get out of control.

It was bad enough that he had to take orders from Luke Lowe for the time being. He was not going to be taking any damned orders from Lowe's woman on the side. This situation he was going to control.

"Now," she breathed.

She was ready, all right. Her nipples, a pale pink shade scarcely darker than the satiny flesh surrounding them, were hard as marble buttons and were as sharply pointed in her excitement as a good many arrow tips he had seen. She spread her long, sleek thighs apart, and he could see moisture beaded in the tight curls of hair around her sex. Her eyes, when she glanced up into his face, were pools of flame. Violet flame. Oh, she was ready all right.

"Make me," he challenged.

She moaned, a furry sound that sprang from deep in her throat. She leaned forward.

With hands and mouth and darting tongue, she engulfed him. Brought him to his tiptoes. Sent his senses reeling.

She slid forward off the edge of the bed, dropped to her knees, and with growling, gobbling, animal sounds began to apply herself wholeheartedly to the task of arousing him even further than he already was.

He felt like he was falling, falling into a warm, damp pit that surrounded his entire body and drenched him in the feel and the scent of superheated woman-flesh. He reached out involuntarily and clutched with one hand for the tall bedpost at the foot of the hotel bed, clutched roughly with the other at the back of her finely molded, patrician head.

He jammed himself deeper into her, and she accepted all of him that way.

Summoning the last reserves of his willpower, Slocum laughed and wrenched himself away from her, leaving her there on her knees with her mouth open and an expression of yearning on her lovely face.

"You're good," he said. His voice, he was both pleased and surprised to note, came out steady and even. It was all he could do to keep from croaking the words into the space that now separated them.

She closed her mouth and smiled. "Have you proven your point yet?"

"Yeah."

Slocum stepped forward. Bent and swept her off the floor into his arms. Gently he turned her fine body, placed her onto the broad bed.

She lifted her arms to him and spread her legs ready to receive him.

With a groan of anticipation, Slocum knelt between her legs and poised himself for the plunge into her.

Meg smiled and reached out to grasp him by the buttocks, her hands clutching hungrily at him, drawing him down, guiding him, demanding his entry.

He had felt the warmth of her mouth before. Now he felt as if he had entered a boiling cauldron as he slid inside the hot, dripping lips of her sex.

He cried out aloud and began to plunge and buck and leap inside her. And the woman matched his every thrust with a hip-driving convulsion of her own.

The universe no longer existed except for that intensely felt portion of it that lay between his knees and his belly. There was no room for any sensations except for this, and the concept of time no longer had meaning. There was only this. There was only now.

The explosion that came—too soon—swept up from his toes and burst outward in an immense outpouring of his entire life-force.

Dimly, he thought he could hear the woman shriek beneath him. Slocum collapsed, uncaring about the weight pressing down on her.

Moments later he stirred, raised himself onto his elbows. He smiled. "So much for the preliminaries. Now let's get down to something serious."

She made a soft, purring noise against the side of his neck and began to stroke his back. "Funny. I'm not at all bored anymore. And now, if you would permit me to take a few liberties, I think I have some really lovely ideas about where we can go from here."

She did.

8

There is very little as boring as a poker game you are not yourself participating in. Or so Slocum decided several hours into Luke Lowe's evening gaming session.

The two had wandered out into the night—Lowe apparently none the wiser about his paramour's afternoon delights—after a heavy meal that did much to restore Slocum's flagging strength. They wound up at a nameless saloon that was scarcely distinguishable from all the others on the main, and only, drag in the young town.

Now, late in the game, Slocum was having to stifle his yawns and make an effort to keep his attention on Lowe and the five other men who sat around the rudely crafted table in a corner of the bar.

Lowe had been winning with monotonous regularity, and Slocum had decided that it was no wonder the man felt he needed a bodyguard. Anyone who cheated with such unimaginative consistency was certain to be spotted sooner or later.

Oh, he was good enough at it. Slocum gave him credit for that much. Lowe could second-deal his stripped deck as well as anyone Slocum had ever

observed. Well enough to work the fancy river-
boats, and that was good indeed.

But the man had no sense of timing at all. None
of the cunning that made a mere cheat into a
genius. A really good cheat, if the term could be
so applied, knew *when* to cheat as well as how. He
could leave his marks hanging on the brink of success, with each turn of each card making them
believe that their own success was just one more
raise away. A really fine cheat could practically
make a mark believe he *was* winning as well as
that he soon would be.

Lowe had none of that ability. The man's phil-
osophy seemed limited to a simple rule: Clean 'em
out right now and make room at the table for the
next sucker.

As far as Slocum was concerned, that was a
damnfool way for a gambling man to make his living. But then that was up to Lowe. Slocum was not
about to advise the man now to ply his trade. Not
as long as he was willing to pay Slocum $50 per
week to make up for his own stupidity. So Slocum
sat, bored, and watched as too large a majority of
the pots found their way into Luke Lowe's hands.

"You aren't playing?" someone asked.

Slocum turned his head, continuing to give
Lowe his attention but grateful for the distraction
of someone to talk to while he did so. "No, I got
pretty thoroughly cleaned out by the Sioux a couple days ago. I'm down to pocket change," he said.

"Say, that's where I seen you before. You was
one of that bunch from the stage that was am-
bushed down the road a ways. Yeah, I seen y'all
come in this morning. Tough shit, eh?"

"Tougher on the ones that didn't walk in with
us," Slocum said. "I ain't complaining about being
alive."

"You got a point there, for a fact," the other man said. He shook his head. "Those stinkin' Sioux. They're gettin' bad anymore. Worse than they was last year, and that's for sure."

"Really?" It was a polite response rather than an interested one, more a way to relieve the boredom than to gain information.

"You bet. We thought everything was gonna be all right, even in spite of Custer's little problems up on the Greasy Grass. The army told us the Sioux and all them others run off up to Canada and wouldn't be around here no more, but somebody seems to of forgot to tell the damned Sioux about that. Some of them has come back. An' there's a lot o' them sporting guns now. A whole helluva lot more than there used to be."

"Really? The bunch we run into wasn't so well armed. Bows and arrows."

"You really was lucky then," the bearded miner said. "Must of been a bunch of youngsters out looking to count coup. Most of the grown-ups these days is better armed than you an' me, I'll tell you. It's gotten so a white man can't hardly work a claim without he has a partner standing guard over his scalp. Real bad, it is. And the bastards have all the ammunition they can shoot up, too. Don't know where all the guns is coming from, but I got me some suspicions."

"Yeah?"

"You bet I do." The miner squinted and cocked his head to the side. "Have you ever heard of some damned heathen Injun stealing a white man's poke after he's kilt him?"

Slocum shook his head. "Taking scalps, sure. But they don't know enough to take the money too."

"Exactly," the miner said triumphantly. "Exactly my point, mister. That's always the way it's been. But not no more. Nowadays when they find some white an' beef him, they take his scalp, sure, but they rob him of his cash an' gold too. Now what does that suggest to you?"

Slocum shrugged.

"Well, I'll tell you what it ought," the miner said, obviously proud of his own reasoning ability. "I'll tell you, for a fact. It says there's white men behind all this. It tells *me* that some white has taken to sellin' the Injuns guns an' ammunition, see, an' he's wanting white man's pay for his goods. That's what it tells me, by damn."

"You could be right," Slocum said thoughtfully.

"Damn straight I'm right. Two an' two generally add up to four. Injuns stealing money from whites an' showing up with rifles an' ammunition, that adds up just as plain. Some white son of a bitch is selling us out. And me and the rest of the boys around here, we'd sure like to get a loop of rawhide around that bastard's balls. Let him do a little of the paying for a change."

"Has there been that much of it, then?"

"Damn straight, there has. A couple boys I've known personally were grassed just last week. Not a half mile from the claims me and my partners have been working. Took, I don't know, better than a thousand dollars from them, the best we can figure. Left behind a mess o' gore that woulda made a buzzard puke, the way they cut on them ol' boys. It was nasty business, let me tell you."

"I believe you," Slocum said. He did, too. There were those who claimed that the Sioux and all the other tribes were noble, misunderstood gentlemen of Nature. As far as Slocum could determine, those folks were all people who had never seen the

body of a white unfortunate enough to have fallen
into angry red hands.

Of course that, in truth, was something of a two-
way street. Slocum had also seen some pretty gory
remains left behind by buffalo hunters and soldiers
and other pissed-off whites who happened to run
across an Indian and decided to play with him before they did their Christian duty by killing him.

All in all, he thought, this business of red versus
white was pretty much a matter of territorial warfare, and each side was going to do as much dam-
age to the other as it could. Motives were a moot
point when it was kill or be killed, and so were
methods. The fellow who came out alive—on either
side—probably had a right to a hard-on for the
blood of the loser.

Besides, none of it was Slocum's affair.

"Say," the miner said, changing the subject, "if
you're down on your luck after that scrap with the
Injuns, I could stand you to a beer or two. I'd be
glad to do it. Figure you'd do the same for me if
the places was switched."

Slocum smiled. "Now that's damn kind of you,
neighbor. I appreciate it. I'm not so bad off,
though. That fella over at the table there, he was
in the scrap with me. He's kind of setting me up
until things look better. I don't want to give you
the idea that I'm in here begging."

The miner waved away any such suggestion.
"It's my pleasure, friend. Really." He turned away
and went to the bar. When he returned he was carrying two heavy schooners of brew. He handed
one to Slocum. "To your good health, scalp an' all."

Slocum drank with him.

"My name's Abner Kraus," he said, wiping a
ring of white foam from his whiskers.

"John . . . Wilse," Slocum said.

"My pleasure, John." Kraus beckoned across the crowded, noisy room, and a moment later he and Slocum were joined by several other miners. Kraus made a round of introductions, and soon Slocum was involved in the friendly banter of a group of hard-working, hard-living miners who were having an evening in town while their partners sat shotgun back at their claims.

Slocum still had to keep an eye on the table where Lowe was plying his dishonest trade, but at least now he was no longer bored.

And these seemed like a cheerful, good-hearted bunch of fellows, Slocum quickly decided. He was much more comfortable in their company than with Lowe. Good old boys, each and every one of them, although their clothing and their accents spoke of backgrounds and home territories from the ends of the nation and some from countries across the salty water.

The evening went much quicker after that, although Slocum had to work at remaining sober enough to do his job in the event Lowe should need the services he was paying for.

9

"Good Lord, woman, don't you ever get enough?" Slocum asked in an exasperated tone of voice.

"No." Her canary-eating smile did not change in the slightest. She was already lying on the soft bed beside him. She arched her back and ran long-nailed fingertips over her large, full breasts and around her perky, pink nipples. "No, I don't seem to get enough of you, John." She smiled. "What is more, I don't think you really want me to." She seemed to feel quite secure about her own undeniable appeal to Slocum or to any other normal male.

"I don't want you to quit, dammit," he said. "But I would like to get some sleep. Occasionally, anyhow."

Meg laughed. "I know, dear. I know."

"Dammit, woman, it ain't funny. Staying up all night baby-sitting your employer and mine, the quick-fingered Mr. Lowe. Then tryin' to keep you satisfied while he's getting the sleep I need every bit as bad as he does. Shit, woman, something's got to give, and I'm afraid it might turn out to be me."

"Poor, poor, John," she said mockingly. "Here. Let me make it feel all better."

"Damn you."

SLOCUM'S GAMBLE 67

With a low-pitched chuckle Meg ceased toying with her own body and rolled onto her side so she could begin toying with Slocum's.

"Mmmm, there. That's nice, John. Yes, there. You like that, don't you?" She giggled. "I can see that you do like it. So do I. Yes. Mmmphfmpth."

"Don't try to talk with your mouth full," Slocum chided. "Didn't your mama never teach you manners?"

She laughed. The sound came out oddly muffled because her mouth was quite full at the time.

After a moment she raised her head and smiled. "See? I _knew_ you were up to it again."

"I wasn't. Reckon maybe I am again at that, though." He tried to look stern but could not quite manage it under the circumstances. After all, she _was_ a beautiful, highly desirable, definitely off-limits female. That was a combination that he always found to be irresistible.

With a smile of his own, John Slocum reached between Meg's thighs and roughly forced her legs apart. Slowly, tantalizingly he began to tweak her clitoris with fingers that were at least as adept at this task as they were in handling the walnut grips and curved hammer of a Colt .45.

Meg rolled onto her back and opened herself to him even more. She began to moan and to writhe beneath his touch, and a moment later she gasped out the intensity of her pleasure.

With a shiver and a sigh she sat up. The haunting look on her lovely face was one of total satisfaction. She bent over him again, raised her head for a moment and said, "It's lost, but I'll bet it isn't gone forever."

"We'll see," Slocum said, affecting a bored tone of voice. The truth was that he was anything but bored by what she was doing. And how *very* well she was doing it.

One of these times he would have to get around to telling her just how very damned good she was. But not for a while. He was afraid any encouragement would just make the damned woman that much more insatiable. Which she already seemed to be. This liaison with Luke Lowe's woman was definitely becoming a problem, albeit a pleasant one. But a fellow had to sleep sometime, didn't he?

"There," she said happily. "That's better. Much better. No, don't. Let me. Yes. Like that. Just lie still now. Yes."

She knelt above him and straddled his hips, lowering herself onto the massive instrument that gave both of them so much pleasure. She skewered herself with his hard flesh and began to rise and fall slowly. She braced herself with her hands spread against his chest and pumped with her eyes wide open, peering down at him as she gauged the pleasure that mounted in his expression, timing her swift, sure movements to match his rising desire until she was flailing his belly with the sharp, angular bones of her pelvis, demanding that his pleasure grow and grow and finally explode within her.

Slocum groaned and released his pent-up breath in a quavering sigh of utter satisfaction. She slowed then, holding him still inside her dripping sex, continuing a slow, smooth stroking that let him fall slowly off the immeasurable peak she had just taken him to.

"Correct me if I'm wrong, John dear, but I believe you might have enjoyed that, even if you were accusing me of its impossibility just a few minutes ago." She laughed.

"Bitch," he said. His tone, though, was gentle, even affectionate.

"Of course. I've never tried to hide that from you."

"Now will you let me get some sleep."

"But of course, dear. If that is what you wanted, why didn't you just say so."

"Bitch," he repeated. He almost meant it this time.

"But of course you are right again." She sighed and lifted her beautiful body from him, allowing him to flop limp and sticky with their mingled juices onto his own flat belly. "I really must get back to my room in case dear Luke should wake up and want some . . . attention."

Slocum laughed. "Attention is it now? I thought you found it a form of amusement."

Meg gave him an unsettling look that he could not quite interpret. "That depends on the circumstances," she said. "And the performers." She smiled, and her expression softened. "In your case, actually, both performer and performance are more than adequate, I would say."

"That's nice to know."

She made a face. "I wish I could say the same about . . . No, never mind. Forget I said anything. All right?"

Slocum shrugged. "Sure." He closed his eyes and reached behind his head to plump up the nearly flat excuse for a pillow the hotel provided to their guests. Damn, but he was tired. Sleep would feel mighty good now.

Yet he could feel a certain amount of tension in the woman's body still beside him on the bed. "Was there something you wanted?" he asked without opening his eyes.

She hesitated, and he thought he could hear

Meg sigh for rather a long time. "No," she said very softly.

"Okay." Deliberately Slocum rolled his head away from her and burrowed into the pillow.

He was still wide-awake and remained so for as long as she was in the room, but she did not need to know that. He felt the tension drain from her, felt her sit on the side of the bed and begin pulling her stockings over those long, lovely, quite perfect legs.

She was giving up rather easily, he thought. He almost laughed at the transparency of her play-acting. She was trying to establish in him a sense of obligation and of sympathy. Trying to build for herself a refuge and an ally. Just in case.

Well, as far as Slocum was concerned, Meg McGee was one hell of a fine lay. But he did not intend to be drawn into any battles on her pretty account. Let her other conquests go for that particular mug's game. Slocum had seen them all, and as much as he might enjoy her in some ways, he did not intend to be taken in by her. After all, gash is only gash, no matter how pretty the package it comes in, and John Slocum was an old boar-hog from way back when it came to the various games not-so-helpless females liked to play when they were being kept by one man and were sleeping with another.

No indeed, not for J. Slocum, that game. No, thank you.

He heard her finish dressing and softly slip out of the room. When she was gone he slid out of the bed himself and padded on silent feet to the door, where he paused for a moment to listen before he slid the bolt home and, finally, went to catch up on some very badly needed sleep.

10

Slocum yawned. Again. Damn, but he wished he could get more sleep than he had been getting lately. And it was still early in the evening, too. Lowe was already at his inevitable card game, was winning just as inevitably. Slocum wondered how long the idiot figured he could get away with such a pointlessly constant scam. The stupid bastard did not seem to realize that a little more time, a more careful attention to detail, and a cardsharp who was that good at cheating his marks could be set for weeks and for thousands in any one likely spot instead of the days and the hundreds that Lowe probably was able to keep his game going.

Not that it was any of John Slocum's business. It was just that sloppiness and ineptitude bothered him. Slocum was a professional himself. He respected professionalism in others, despised weakheaded louts, no matter what particular profession was involved. Even in cheating at cards, Slocum liked to see it done well and properly or not at all. Luke Lowe simply did not deserve John Slocum's respect. The man was a fine mechanic, a poor thinker. Piss on him. Slocum would use him and would take his money for as long as was necessary. Not for an hour longer.

"Hello, John."

"Good evening, Abner." Kraus had joined him. This too had become a habit, an every-evening event to be expected. But the miner's appearance was something Slocum looked forward to. The man was open and friendly. He was just plain likable. And Slocum suspected that he was also a damned good placer miner. Not everyone could make that claim, and even fewer would be truthful if they did. Kraus did not make it himself, but Slocum suspected the truth of it anyway. If nothing else, Abner Kraus always had a supply of yellow dust in his leather poke. That must be indicative of something.

"How are you this evening, John?"

"Fine. You look a bit down at the mouth, though. What's wrong?"

Kraus did look unhappy, agitated. His normally smiling mouth was drawn into a frown, and worry creased the portions of his face that showed above his full beard. "Those stinking Sioux again, John. I tol' you already what a problem they been around here, an' they're at it again. They come down on a couple camps the next drainage over from our'n. We could hear the shootin' goin' on something fierce over there. Jesus Christ, man, I ain't heard so much gunfire since Shiloh."

Slocum nodded understandingly. He had heard that same thunder of burning powder. He knew. For a fleeting moment he wondered which color uniform Abner Kraus had been wearing when he heard those battle sounds. But Slocum as quickly put the question aside. It no longer mattered. That was yesterday's war. Today and tomorrow's survival were the things that mattered now.

"When we heard all that," Kraus went on glumly, "we naturally figgered it was the white boys

that was doing all that shootin'. Seemed only likely, you know?" He seemed to be asking for Slocum's approval as well as his comprehension.
Automatically Slocum nodded his agreement.

"Anybody would've figgered the same," Kraus
insisted, more to himself than to Slocum. "Come
to find out, b'damn, that we was wrong, though. It
was them stinkin' red nigger Sioux that was doing
all that powder-burning, not those poor boys on
their lawful claims. The damned Injuns shot them
up so bad it looked afterward like those boys'd
been killed with shotguns. But me an' my partners
was able to hear it. Those was rifles, surer than
hell they was. I'd swear to it. But them Injuns,
they just poured it on an' on an' wouldn't quit.
Must of shot up a thousand rounds of ammunition,
I tell you. They wasn't the least bit worried about
running out. Must have the stuff by the case."

Kraus sighed. "It's gettin' worse out here all
the time now, John. Gets much worse'n it already
is, we might all of us be drove off our claims, be
drove plumb down the rail line and out of these
hills entire."

"Isn't that the general idea of the thing?"

"I s'pose it is, from them red bastards' point
of view, come to think of it. I swear, I wisht I
could get my hands on the miserable white bastard that's been selling them those guns an' all that
ammunition. I'd give him an idear of what he's
caused all these decent boys out here. I would for
a fact."

Another miner still encrusted with dried muck
from his placer claim turned from a conversation
he had been having nearby. "I heard that," the
man said, "and I second your motion, sir. If you
have any inkling at all of where we might find the
perpetrator I would be glad to join your vigilance

movement and commence the hostilities with castration. Using a stone knife, at that." The man sounded like he meant it.

Others crowded close to the discussion that was now well under way, and Abner repeated for them several times the tale of new woe that had befallen those miners on their claims.

To Kraus's credit, Slocum noted, the story got no larger in the retelling, and Abner's estimate of the amounts of ammunition expended did not rise with the number of beers the storyteller had consumed. It became obvious that, right or wrong, the man was recounting a figure that he genuinely believed to be accurate. And he was, from whichever side of the war, an old soldier who just might know what he was talking about.

If that was true, Slocum reflected, things could get in a real ball-buster of a bind around the Deadwood strike. The place was set way the hell and gone away from civilized society. Hell, it had been only four years or so since the first military expedition had explored it—led, ironically enough, by the same George Custer who later died at the hands of the same Indian nations he had stirred into frenzy by way of his explorations and gold discovery.

Anyway, Slocum realized, they were one hell of a long ways from the nearest town, the nearest railroad, even from the nearest navigable river.

If the whole bloody Sioux Nation should happen to be encouraged by the successes of those few that had stayed behind on American soil, if they should decide to come boiling back down out of Canada and have another crack at the white interlopers on their sacred Black Hills . . . Jesus, Slocum thought. With or without a heavy new supply of guns for those bastards, this whole area and every white-skinned miner in or near it could wake up dead some fine morning. John Slocum among them. Not a dandy thought.

Slocum scratched his chin speculatively. He sure wouldn't mind it when he got his stake together and could get the hell out of here.

In the meantime he had work to do. Of sorts. Time to put in, anyway. He accepted another schooner of beer from Abner and listened to the growing concern of the honest miners who had joined into the conversation.

They were all plenty worried, Slocum realized. They might well have good reason to be.

11

"You look bored, my friend," Kraus said. He laughed. "Again. It seems to be becoming an occupational hazard with you these days."

"I cain't argue with you over it," Slocum responded.

"And where is your worthy employer, the gentleman Lowe?" Kraus was still laughing. It was no secret that he was less than fond of the gambler. Kraus, like Slocum himself, thought Luke Lowe to be about as much a gentleman as a boar hog was.

"Damned if I know," Slocum told him honestly enough. "The sonuvabitch said he was taking off for a couple days. Though where a man could go around here in the two or three days Lowe said he'd be gone, well, damned if I know. I reckon he just wanted a break from the rigors of the tables. Or something. He was kinda secretive about it, come to think of it. Not that I care. It means I've got a few days to myself. With pay. And I can use the sleep."

"You'll get fat and lazy if you lie around sleeping day and night," Kraus accused.

Pussy-whipped was more like it, Slocum thought, but he did not think it a good idea to say so. He was enjoying his break from Lowe's cheating all night every night, but he was not at all sure he could survive several days of the McGee woman day and now nightlong too.

"Actually," Slocum said, "I wouldn't mind getting out of this damn gulch myself for a few days. But I don't know where the hell a man would go, like I told you."

Kraus grinned. "In that case, by God, I got a hell of a fine idea, John."

"Share it, an' I'll see what I think of it too."

"You bet," the smiling miner said. "Me and a couple of the boys've been thinking about looking for another placer claim. Most of the really good claims anywhere close in are already turning into hardrock claims, and that isn't the way my friends and I like to go. So we thought we'd look around a little further out again, see if we can come up with something better than what we're working now. So my question, John, and my invitation, is: do you know anything about placer mining?"

Slocum grinned. "I'll tell you the truth, Abner. I don't know shit about placer mining. But I wouldn't mind watching someone who does know what he's doing. And if there was any trouble I could at least add my gun to the noise."

Kraus looked more serious. "Aye, trouble. There's been enough of that around here of late. We could use all the firepower we can find. And of course if we find gold, a share of it would be yours."

"No need for that," Slocum protested. "I told you, I don't know shit about placer mining. I couldn't be much help to you from that end of it."

"And I told *you*. If we make a find, a share will be yours. That's the way we do things, y'see. Fair for one and fair for all."

"Well I'll be a son of a bitch," Slocum said with a grin. "I might become a rich man yet, in that case."

Kraus was still sober, however. "You know the likelihood of that, John Wilse. And like I said, there's been more than enough trouble hereabouts. The Sioux are acting pure crazy these days, and a man never knows in the morning what the state of his hair will be that night. I could be asking you to join us in death, you know."

"Bullshit," Slocum said happily. "And now that you've asked me, I'm damn sure going along, Indians or no Indians. Hell, if I didn't go with you boys, Abner, I might take a nap in the sun in front of the hotel over there tomorrow, an' some fool would come along and dump a load o' lumber on me by accident. I figure when my time's up I'm dead, and that'll be that."

Besides, Slocum thought to himself, Luke Lowe might be a fine hand as a cheat and Abner Kraus might be a hell of a placer miner, but when it came to gunplay, John Slocum was a master of the trade. If there was any trouble coming, those good ol' boys would be a lot better off if Slocum was with them than if he was back in Deadwood cooling coffee. Or screwing the McGee. And anyway, it would be a welcome break from the monotony of the camp.

"I'm accepting your invitation, and that's that," Slocum said with finality.

"Good enough, John. We'll leave at the break of dawn then."

"I'll be ready."

The miner was as good as his word or a little bit better. Kraus and four other men Slocum recognized from Abner's crowd of friends were knocking on Slocum's hotel door well before dawn the next morning.

"Get your ass dressed, Wilse," they told him good-naturedly. "We don't allow no naked men in a gold-hunting party."

"There's a *strong* superstition against it," another said.

Slocum dressed and slung his Colt into place, put on his hat, and stamped his way into his boots. He was ready in moments. "Waitin' on you," he told them.

They traveled several hours north and east from Deadwood, and at least half that time they were never out of sight of at least one claim that was already being actively worked, with whatever degree of success for the claim owners.

No wonder, Slocum thought, the Sioux were so pissed off at the number of whites who had invaded this sacred territory that was supposed to be theirs forever by the terms of a government treaty.

Everywhere you looked there were shacks and diggings and white men to populate them. The country was positively crawling with activity. Activity both white and red. Slocum could see the incredible amount of white activity as they rode; the red activity he had seen enough of back there on the road. And there had been still more since then, according to the reports in town. It was a bad situation, and Slocum could understand both sides of it. The Sioux resented the intrusion of the whites; the whites were just as passionate in their desire to grab up the gold they knew to be lying in the streams and hillsides here. Neither side was likely to back off from their own desires, and as always when two different groups are dead set on holding to a collision course, there is damned sure going to be a collision.

Even after they were beyond the circle around Deadwood where claims were being actively worked, though, Kraus and his partners continued to ride, passing by one stream after another where Slocum would have expected them to stop and look for the precious metal that had brought them here from wherever their distant homes once had been.

They passed one creekbed after another that looked identical to those already being worked, as far as Slocum's untrained eye could tell. If there was gold in that stream back there, why not in this one here, he wondered.

Finally he gave up wondering and asked.

Kraus gave him a look that, however kindly, implied that Slocum had not been lying when he disclaimed any expertise as a placer miner.

"Ride over there, John. Yeah. Right into the stream now. Forward a few more steps. Forward. Uh huh. Stop there."

Slocum did as he was instructed. His borrowed horse, supplied by Abner, splashed through the shallow, swift-running stream and threw up a spray of icy droplets that dampened and cooled Slocum's lower legs. The horse stood in the stream where Kraus had told Slocum to draw rein and patiently lowered its head to snort and drink and paw the burbling water.

"Look down by your left foot now, John. That's right. Look just in front o' the toe of your boot. What do you see?"

Slocum shrugged. "Water, Abner. I see running water there, same as anywhere else along this stretch of nothing."

The rest of the men began to laugh. Abner did too, but patiently he explained, "John, I know nobody's likely ever told you this before, but gold don't float." He grinned. "Underneath the water, that's where you want to look. Now what do you see?"

Slocum tried again. It was difficult trying to read the streambed gravel under the swiftly moving surface with its ever-changing patterns of ripple and reflection, but he did as he was told. A man never ought to argue with a fellow who was an expert, he knew.

"Pea gravel, of course. Some rock. A little sand or light dirt. The usual crap."

"Any black mud?" Abner asked.

"Nope."

"That's right. There's no black mud. Mind now, it don't always work this way, but most generally you'll find gold, placer gold anyway, associated with black mud that contains a lot of iron in the mineralization. Matter of fact, most of the time you can pick up the mud with a magnet if you happen to have one handy. Where you find that black mud, you just might find gold. Remember that."

Slocum nodded. Good as he was at what he did, there were still some areas where he could get an education.

"Now what else do you see, John?"

"I don't see any black mud, that's for sure, and . . . well, shit. Why didn't I notice that before? There's a depression in the streambed, and there's no rock or fall or anything upstream to've caused it. It's kind of a hole in the bed that's got no reason to be there." He glanced up at Abner and his friends sitting on their horses on the bank above him. "Is that what you wanted me to see?"

Kraus grinned. "Uh huh. That hole, it didn't get there by itself. Somebody come along and dug it.

Which means that this section here has been picked over already. And if there was any color worth planning, it's already been claimed. It hasn't been claimed. Which means we got a ways to ride yet."

"Well I'll be a double-dipped son of a bitch," Slocum said cheerfully.

"Prob'ly," Abner agreed. "Now if you'll haul that poor, long-sufferin' pony of yours outta the cold water, John, we will get on with the business of making us all rich men."

12

Slocum was thinking about the last time he was down in the old smuggler's port of Galveston on the Gulf coast of Texas. There was a wharf there and off to the west from it a long string of tidal flats where, when the tide was just right, youngsters of the town would wade out with the nets that they would cast and haul back endlessly as they waded through the shallow, warm salt water. If they were lucky they would bring in fish that they could sell for pocket money.

While Slocum was there he'd been sitting on a cotton bale on the wharf, enjoying a cigar and idly watching four of the kids working their nets. The boys had gotten into a splashing contest, the way kids will do when they aren't accomplishing anything else, and the commotion they were making apparently stirred up a sand shark.

The boys hadn't seen the ugly predator in the murky water they had created with their horseplay, and the thing had put a hell of a gash in the foot of one of the boys. The fishermen who'd pulled the boys to safety said the little shark probably got confused in the mud and thought the flash of the boy's foot was a fish, else it would not have struck him. Slocum had been willing to take their word for it. Like placer mining, that was something that was not exactly in his field of knowledge.

What brought it to mind now, several years and several thousand miles away, was this fucking business of placer mining. Shee-it, he thought. If some damned shark had crept up the Mississippi and then up to Missouri and then up the Belle Fourche and then up whatever the hell this stinking little ice-water creek was, why, the little son-uvabitch could snap John Slocum's foot plumb off at the ankle.

And Slocum would most probably never know it had happened until he tried to walk out of the bitchin' creek. His feet, his ankles, every damn thing from the knees down had gone completely numb. Hours ago, it seemed like. And his back. Good Christ, it felt like it was already busted and was ready to snap in two at any time. Without warning.

This whole fucking business of placer mining had, so far, about the same appeal as picking cotton. The only difference was that with the placer mining a man didn't even get wages for his work. *Shee-it!*

Slocum stood upright, groaning, and arched his back. He reached around with a hand that was fish-belly white and wrinkled from immersion in the cold water and tried to massage the small of his back.

"What's the matter, John?" one of Abner's friends called out. The man—his name was Ned—was grinning.

Oddly enough, none of them except Slocum seemed particularly bothered by the ball-breaking stoop labor they were so cheerfully subjecting themselves to while they stood knee deep in cold

water. Used to it, Slocum told himself with no
particular satisfaction. He considered himself to
be in more than fair shape, and yet these miners
were working his ass off and never showing a hint
of strain themselves.

The way they were working it, all of them except Abner were operating the pans, while Abner
used a short-handed spade to keep the rest of them
busy with fresh gravel. Abner dug load after load
of muck and small gravel from the streambed and
dumped his treasures into the other men's pans
so they could swirl and wash it with those smooth,
practiced flicks of their wrists—Slocum's being
somewhat less smooth and infinitely less practiced, even after hours at the chore—to float away
the lighter rock and sand and dirt and, hopefully,
to leave any gold behind.

So far neither Slocum nor anyone else had
found any gold. But Slocum had made a few dis-
coveries. The way they were doing the washing required the men on the pans to stand in the water,
bent over so the edges of the pans were just barely
clear of the moving surface. With a slight adjust-
ment to the position of the pan they could take on
more water, swirl unwanted liquid out, or wash
the whole mess into the creek.

It was efficient as far as the washing was concerned, but it did require the panner to assume
that bent-over, back-breaking position and to hold
it for as long as he was working.

Slocum had thought for a time that he had
found a dandy way to improve on their system.
Like everyone else in this country and in half the
known world besides, John Slocum had seen all
those woodcut prints in the papers and the maga-
zines and such showing placer miners at work in
the gold fields of California. An entire generation

had grown up by now on tales of the forty-niners, and Slocum had not escaped all the hoopla that went with those stories. Nobody could have. And at least half of the woodcuts Slocum had ever seen showed a bearded miner in a slouch hat kneeling beside—not in, damn it, but beside—a pretty mountain brook with a placer pan in his hands.

How these boys could have escaped seeing those prints Slocum did not know, but it was perfectly obvious that the way to pan for gold was not to stand stupidly out in the middle of a lot of liquid ice; it was to kneel dry and happy beside the shit.

Right. You bet. Slocum had tried it.

Shee-it. Whoever had created all those stinking woodcuts hadn't been much of a placer miner, Slocum damn soon decided. For one thing, you still broke your fucking back from leaning forward to reach the water you had to have to wash and separate and clean the pan. Except that then you had to lean forward as well as down, and worry about keeping your balance, and there was even *more* strain on your aching back than there would have been if you were standing out there like Abner's friends were doing.

And if that weren't bad enough, you still got wet from kneeling beside the stream, if only because to wash a pan of gravel right you had to swirl the slop inside and you got water on you from the thighs down. You were still wet and damn cold, if not quite so much so.

But worst of all, when you kneel on gravel and stream-side rocks the little bastards do their utmost to try to cut your knees into raw, bloody ribbons. Slocum would have sworn that each and every pebble in Dakota Territory was trying its level best to work its way inside his kneecaps and roost there with a stony smile.

Bad as standing in the damned water was, kneeling beside it was way the the hell worse. Whoever had made all those woodcuts, Slocum decided, was one stupid son of a bitch. He sighed and rubbed the small of his back and accepted another spadeful of gravel from Abner.

"How long are we going to keep this up?" he asked.

Abner grinned. "Until we're rich."

Slocum shook his head. "That long, huh?" He began to wash the fresh load of shit Kraus had given him.

Swish and swirl, wash out the big stuff; swish and swirl, separate the small stuff; swish and swirl, float some of it out; do it all over again, and . . .

"My God, boys, I've got something here!" Slocum yelled.

Right there, right-fucking-there, right beside that riffle cast into the sloping side of his pan, right there was a hint of bright yellow. He was positive of it. Absolutely positive.

Abner splashed to his side within seconds, and all of the others stopped working. They stood with their pans in their hand waiting for Abner Kraus to check the newcomer's find.

Slocum held the pan up to waist level and pointed. "If that ain't gold, Abner, I'll French kiss your hairy ass."

He was excited. No question about it. There was a thrill running through him unlike anything he had ever felt before. This was more purely exciting, by God, than peeling the door off a Wells Fargo safe and finding a thousand, hell, *ten* thousand times that amount of gold that had been refined and smelted and melted into gold coin.

It was the biggest kick John Slocum could remember since he had first discovered pussy, and he was grinning from ear to red-flushed ear.

"Well, dammit, Abner, it *is* gold, isn't it?" he demanded.

Abner chuckled and probed the remaining muck in Slocum's pan with a work-roughened fingertip. "Oh, it's gold all right, John. Damn sure is."

"Well?"

Kraus laughed. "We've all been finding little bits of float dust like that, John. The other boys, they've been getting that here an' there right along."

"You're kidding me."

Abner shook his head. "No, but I reckon it does mean one thing. I mean, color like that ain't worth panning for. That's maybe three cents worth in that pan you're holding, John. I doubt it's more than that." He clapped Slocum on the shoulder. "But it does mean you're starting to get the hang of how to pan for it, John. It sure does mean that." Kraus turned to the others. "Get back to it, boys. We still aren't halfway far enough upstream, I reckon."

Slocum shook his head.

Kraus began to turn away from him, but he stopped where he was in the cold, running stream and gave Slocum a warm smile.

"Tell me something, John."

"Uh huh?"

"You got a hell of a boot out of it, didn't you?"

Slocum laughed. "I admit it, Abner. I did for a fact."

"In case you've been wondering, that right there, John, that's why we put up with all this hard work an' horseshit day after day. It just plain does something to a man's guts when he turns color in his pan. Better'n anything I've ever known before.

Better'n a bottle or a woman or any other damn thing a human person could ever hope to know. And that, that's what placer mining is all about."

Slocum sighed and bent to wash out his pan. But not, by damn, before he very carefully extracted each of the tiny grains of gold dust with his fingernails and carefully deposited the few specks inside a twist of paper he fashioned from a cigar band.

Those specks might not be worth anything to Abner Kraus and his professional mining friends, but they were gold, by God, and they belonged to John Slocum. Very personally.

He got back to work.

13

"What was . . . ?"

"Shut up," Slocum hissed. The big Colt was in his hand as he flowed swiftly to his feet, and he motioned the miners to remain where they were.

Abner Kraus and his friends might know a hell of a lot more than Slocum when it came to panning gold, but this, by God, was John Slocum's neck of the woods.

"But what . . . ?" one of them began to protest.

"Shut up, I told you," Slocum said in a low voice. He was still straining to listen. "That's gunfire. Not far away, either." He paused. "At least twenty men firing, I'd say. Maybe more." He looked at Abner. "There could be a bunch of prospectors over there trying to hold off some Sioux. The way I see it we got two choices. Get the hell out of here before the Indians know we're around. Or see if we can help. I reckon you're in charge here Abner, so you decide."

"You're sure?" Kraus asked.

Slocum shrugged. "Who's *sure*? I'm just telling you what's likely. I s'pose it could be a bunch of drunks having target practice. Or a band of mountain men that don't know the rendezvous died out a long time ago. All I can tell you from standing here is that there's a lot of guns going off some-where over in that direction." He hooked a thumb past the ridge top that rose abruptly to the west of the creek-side meadow where they had been hav-ing their lunch.

Slocum squinted toward the sun, already well on its way down past the midday zenith. "We have plenty of time to take it either way. It won't be dark for hours yet."

"There's no question, John," Kraus said. "Get your guns, boys. And I think from here on we should follow Wilse here as our leader. Agreed?"

The miners took no time arguing or complain-ing, Slocum saw. They began to gather up their horses and weapons without delay, and one of them kicked apart the fire they had been drying off beside.

"Next time it might be us needin' help," one of the men mumbled as he pulled his cinches tight.

"Any of you boys been in the cavalry?" Slocum asked. He got nothing from them in response but a lot of shaking heads. "The army then?" All ex-cept Ned nodded.

"That's something, anyway," he told them. "Ned, you hang back and watch the rest of us." He grinned. "If you see me hunt for a hole to crawl into, you'll know you'd better do the same. The rest of you, trail along behind me. Far enough to give you a good jump if I blunder into trouble but close enough you don't lose sight of me. We aren't going to try anything fancy no matter what's going on over there. If it's what it sounds like, I'll take a good look and then come back to talk it over with you before I get you into a fight. All right?"

All of them agreed.

Slocum hoped they remembered that when the

time came. One idiot in a firefight can ruin a
man's whole day. "Let's go then."

He swung onto the borrowed horse and led them
in a series of switchbacks up the side of the slope
above. Any of the horses could probably have
made it up in a direct scramble, but Slocum knew
better than to wear out the mounts of his command before a moment of absolute necessity.

And, by God, for the time being this ragtag collection of placer miners was a command of sorts.
Outlaw he might be, but once upon a time he had
been a leader of armed and mounted men who
were respected for who and what they were, and
after the passage of years it felt good once again
to have the feeling he did when he rode at the
head of an armed body. Not leading a pack of
outlaws who might legitimately be gunned down
by any passing posse but leading a group who had
the strength of right on their side. It felt . . . nice.
He sat straighter in his saddle, and his right hand
opened and closed in search of a curved saber that
no longer was at his side.

He sighed and could not suppress a brief grin.
There were three men back there who admitted
to army service in the past. The odds were that at
least two of them and maybe all three had worn
blue coats instead of gray. Still, they were better
than nothing, and for a fleeting moment there he
had been able to remember things that he had
thought long forgotten.

"Drop back now, but keep me in sight," he said
as his horse breasted the top of the rise and he
stopped below the skyline to study the next gulch
before exposing them all to the view of anyone
who might be lurking in the bottom below this
ridge.

Following both his ears and his instinct for self-preservation, Slocum led the miners not directly toward the sounds of battle—which continued to wax and wane as they rode, sometimes swelling to a furious volume and again dying down to a few sporadic shots—but northward around the end of the next ridge.

The gunfire was coming from someplace very close now but beyond the next ridge, and Slocum had a choice. He could bring his tiny relief force to the scene over the ridge, which would of necessity skylight them there, or he could approach the battleground from an end of the gulch where the fighting seemed to be taking place.

Since surprise might be more important than the superior position of the higher ground—and, mostly, because his instincts ordered him to do so —Slocum chose to go around rather than over.

He looked back at one point and was pleased to see that Abner and the other men were doing exactly as he had told them. They had spaced themselves about two hundred yards to his rear and were riding with their Winchesters across their saddlebows. Good men, Slocum thought. He grinned. Or ignorant. There had been a time or two in the past when his eager troopers had been unable to contain themselves and had blown good planning with their lust for the excitement of the charge. Slocum would have understood, if not approved, had these miners decided to go busting up and over in relief of their fellow miners on the other side of that ridge.

Forget those boys behind you, Slocum reminded himself. You won't do them or anybody else any damn good if you go waltzing into the middle of a pack of Sioux around this point of rock.

He stopped his horse and with hand signals ordered the others to remain where they were while Abner rode forward to join him.

"What I want you to do," Slocum whispered when Kraus had reached his side, "is to hold my horse. There ain't much shooting going on right now, but they aren't much more'n three hundred yards away. Just the other side of this rock and back down a little ways, if I'm reading the terrain right. I want to climb up there—I'll be in sight of you all the way—and take a look before we ride in there. I'll know better what we ought to do when I get back down." He grinned. "If I come down runnin' like hell you can take it as a sign to turn your horse around, Abner. But I'd appreciate it if you was to leave mine here before you throw iron to yours."

"Whatever you say." Kraus—indeed all of them, as far as Slocum could determine—seemed intent on helping where he was needed, but he was also steady and willing to listen.

Kraus took the reins, and Slocum began the short scramble up the spine of rock here where the ridge petered out. Slocum left his Winchester on his saddle. He would not need long-range firepower until or unless the whole group of them was in position. And he might well want speed and mobility on his way back down.

Slocum picked his way cautiously to the top and removed his broad-brimmed hat before edging up the last few inches. If any Sioux were on the other side of that chunk of rock, he would just as soon not advertise his presence. He crawled into position beside the base of a boulder and looked around.

There were Sioux down there, all right. He could see a band of them, all painted up and looking fierce as hell, less than a hundred yards from

where he lay watching. The Indians were dis-
mounted and—he swiveled his eyes slowly through
the dense growth below him—several very young-
looking warriors had been detailed to hold the
horses of the fighting crowd.

Very efficient, Slocum thought. It looked like
the Sioux had been taking some lessons from the
yellowleg troopers they'd been fighting with for
the past dozen years or so.

The Sioux had formed an almost military-look-
ing skirmish line, too, and were lying across the
floor of the gulch using rocks and brush and, over
there, a dead horse to shield them from the
miners.

So the Indians would be between the miners and
Slocum's party if Slocum decided to lead them in.
Which might not be such a drawback if they came
in screaming with their Colts blasting and the
shock of surprise to immobilize the Sioux long
enough to let the miners get close. If things were
right they could catch the Sioux in a cross fire and
have a regular turkey shoot, Slocum was thinking.

He was concentrating so hard on the best line
of attack that for a moment it did not dawn on
him that he as yet had no idea how far this magnificent charge was going to carry them before
they reached the embattled whites beyond. It had
been a hell of a while since he'd been thinking in
terms like this, Slocum reminded himself. Slow
down, boy, or you'll get the whole fucking crowd
killed.

He examined the narrow gulch floor beyond the
line of Sioux. The brush was fairly thick down
there, and the angle he was viewing it from was
too shallow for ideal observation. He would have
done better if he had climbed the ridge lane oppo-

site the place where Abner's friends were now waiting for him.

There.

He could see a faint puff of gunsmoke rise from behind a blowdown, and closer to Slocum one of the Sioux ducked as a spray of gravel and rock chips was flung into his face.

There had been little firing these past few minutes, but now the whole pack of Sioux came to their knees and began to pour lead down the length of the gulch.

Slocum hoped the defenders were well dug in. If they did not have cover from that bullet-wasting fusillade they were going to be in trouble. On the other hand, if they did not have cover at least as good as the Sioux had taken they would already have been in trouble, and there would have been no time for Slocum and the other miners to reach them.

Sure enough, a wall of drifting white smoke began to rise from the position near where Slocum had seen that first gunshot. Whoever was down there, and it looked like a dozen guns or more were firing, they were well entrenched behind their cover.

They damn sure had cartridges to burn, too, Slocum saw. The fire was so heavy Slocum would have busted some asses if any of the boys in his old command had wasted ammunition like that, and they just kept pouring it on.

Both sides were shooting now like they had all the ammo in the world and were trying to turn their Winchesters into Gatlings just to get rid of it all. And neither side was much for accuracy, Slocum saw. Since he had crawled up here he hadn't yet seen one casualty, and some of the bullets from the other end were buzzing within hearing distance of Slocum's hidden position.

If those miners were that bad at their shooting it was a wonder they'd kept their hair long enough to reach the Black Hills, he thought.

Still, they sure as hell needed help, and it was about time he crawled back out of here and organized Abner and his pals into a rescue party. Those idiots down at the other end of the gulch looked like they could use some straight-shooting support from any source they could find.

Slocum reached back to grab his hat and prepared to slither back down the slope to his horse. He knew exactly the way he wanted to work this now, exactly the line of attack he would take to punch through that Sioux skirmish line and reach the . . .

Gawdalmighty!

One of the Sioux managed a good shot, if only by accident, and down on the other side his target bucked convulsively to his feet with half his jaw shot away. A renewed flurry of Sioux shots picked the man up and held him dancing like a marionette in the hands of a man with palsy, until half his body was running with blood and finally he dropped out of sight.

Slocum very nearly raised up into plain sight from trying to watch the dead man fall, though. And what he was watching was not the death itself—he had seen too many men die, had killed too many himself, for the sight to be a source of amazement now. What he could scarcely believe was that the man those Sioux had shot into so many small pieces was—Slocum could scarcely believe it even after having seen it for himself— another damned Sioux Indian.

"What the . . . ?" he whispered.

He crept back from the skyline and raced back along the ridge until he judged he was far enough to get a better look at what was going on below.

When he wormed back into position this time he could see both lines of fighters: two bands of warriors stripped to loincloths and paint. *And both of them were Sioux.*

This made no sense at all.

Slocum lay on the peak of the ridge and searched the bullet-tattered ground between the two lines of warriors. There was no sign of any whites. No entrenched miners battling for their lives. No sign that there had ever been a white man's boot set onto the soil that separated those two lines of Indians.

It was crazy as hell.

Yet, Slocum remembered, there was no mistake here. There was no chance that one band did not know they were fighting other Sioux.

When that warrior had raised up in his pain, the entire skirmish line of the Sioux opposing his band had drawn down on him and blown him to rags. They *knew* they were fighting other Indians. *Had* to know it.

But why ... ?

Slocum could not understand it, not in the slightest. Not that an uninformed white was ever likely to understand Sioux thinking in the best of times. But this, this was incredible.

He was shaking his head.

He was also getting the hell out of there.

Slocum began to work his way carefully down the slope toward Ned and the other miners, motioning to Abner as he went for Kraus to bring his horse and come pick him up.

By damn, if those Sioux wanted to fight it out and exterminate each other, they were welcome to it. As far as Slocum was concerned this was one fight he would walk wide of.

For a change he was right willing to see the ugly sights of Deadwood once again. And for that matter, Abner could keep his placer mining too. That was a game John Slocum did not particularly want to play. The hours were too long, the work too hard, and the pay too small. John Slocum had had his thrill now. He'd be glad to get back to the lamplights and Meg McGee this night, by God.

And the crazy-assed Sioux could just go right on shooting each other. Slocum couldn't understand them; he wasn't even going to try.

"You ain't gonna believe this, boys," he said as he neared the waiting miners, "so take a grain o' salt and listen to what I got to say. But let's get to riding while I do the talking. We don't wanta be here when them boys on the other side of the hill get done shooting hell outta each other."

14

"John."

"Yes, Abner?" It was yet another evening, another day gone by with too little sleep and—he could hardly believe he would ever think such a thing—perhaps a bit too much pussy for comfort. More of the same old shit. Slocum was bored. But as always he was glad to see Kraus. "How about a beer? On me this time."

Kraus shook his head impatiently. "Later maybe. Have you, uh, got a minute?"

"For you? Of course." Slocum led the way into a corner of the saloon where they were not so likely to be overheard. Kraus seemed to want to talk to him about something serious, and Slocum could keep an eye on Lowe's poker game from across the room as easily as over the man's shoulder. The Colt at Slocum's hip did not much care what distance was involved, so long as Slocum did his part. "Indian trouble, Abner?"

Kraus shook his head impatiently. "No, it's not the crazy Sioux. I'm afraid it involves you."

Slocum's eyebrows went up, and he waited for his friend to continue.

"Look, John," Kraus said uncertainly, "you an' me . . . we get along pretty good, you know?"

Slocum nodded. "I'd say so."

"Yeah." Abner looked uncomfortable. "Yeah, well, the thing is, I figure you're an honest sort, in your own way."

"To tell you the truth, I figure you are too."

"An' I don't figure . . . ah, hell, John." The man looked miserable now. "You're hangin' close to this Lowe fella. That's pretty plain, you see. He's staking you an' all. Maybe even hiring you?" It was clearly voiced as a question, although Abner Kraus had long since proven himself to be a man who was sensitive to the privacy of others. He had never before asked Slocum anything that might be considered to be of a personal, private nature. He would not have done so now, Slocum realized, without some compelling reason.

"Maybe," Slocum said noncommittally.

Kraus looked pained. "Looka here, John, I happen to know . . . an' I wasn't prying, mind . . . I wouldn't do that . . . don't really give a shit what a man wants to call himself. I just overheard some talk one time, you see. . . ."

"Go on, Abner. We know each other well enough that I'm not going to take any offense, if that's what you're worried about here."

Kraus looked a little bit more at ease, although not much. "That's part of it, true. Part of it. But you see, John, I got some real good friends in this camp. Boys I've really come to like. I don't want to see none of them hurt. Don't want to see you hurt either. You know what I mean?"

"No, I don't think I do, Abner."

"Yeah, well . . ." Kraus dropped his eyes away from Slocum's face and peered toward his boot toes. "The thing is, I happen to know what your name really is. I've, uh, I reckon I've heard of you before. Stuff that may or may not be true. But also, which I figure is God's own truth, I've also heard that you're hell on iron wheels when it comes to gun trouble. You know?"

Slocum shrugged. "A man does what he has to do to keep breathing. I won't deny that. Where'd you hear my name, anyhow?"

"A, uh, a girl. Down in one o' the cribs. She didn't pay any particular attention to what she was sayin'. Didn't seem to of heard about you before. She was just mentionin' havin' been caught out by a bunch of red Injuns with Lowe—you know how I'm always harpin' about them red niggers anyhow, which is how it come up—an' she was saying how she'd been caught out in that coach, an' how a fella name of Slocum had come along and helped get her outta there."

"Miss Porter?" Slocum asked incredulously. "Miss Jennifer Porter? Jesus."

"I don't know about the Porter part. She calls herself Jenny, though."

Slocum shook his head. And to think, he had taken a crib girl for a dressmaker or some other prim, spinsterish type. How wrong could one man get?

"It's no big deal, anyway," Kraus assured him. "I never made no fuss about it, an' I doubt that she'd think it important enough to mention to anybody."

"Is that what you wanted to tell me, Abner? I mean, hell, I don't care about my friends knowing who I am."

Abner shook his head. "No, dammit, that ain't really it, John. I'm just kinda working up to it, if you know what I mean. Just kinda setting the stage. Like I said, I like you an' I like a bunch of other ol' boys around here, an' if there's any way I can see to avoid it I'd sure like to keep you an' them from having to lock horns and butt heads. You know?"

"Not yet, but I hope I'm fixing to. Go on."

"Yeah, well . . ." Kraus looked uncomfortable again. "Some of the boys are starting to get suspicious of this gambler fella Lowe. An' if you're siding him, if maybe you was obligated to back him in case o' trouble, well, I just think it could go awful hard on some mighty good boys. Now do you understand?"

"Oh." Slocum pursed his lips and blew out a long breath. "Maybe I do at that, Abner. Maybe I do at that."

"I don't want there to be trouble betwixt fellas that I know an' like, John. I really would hate to see that."

"So would I, Abner. So would I." Slocum paused. "Do I have some time to be thinking on this? Or are they fixing to brace Lowe with their suspicions?"

Kraus fidgeted. He seemed to be thinking.

That was reasonable, Slocum knew. Abner would want to weigh anything he might say, looking for the conflicts and the loyalties involved, *before* he said anything at all. Once spoken, a word or a warning could not be recalled, and in something like this it would not do to protect one while harming the other. A good and honest man like Kraus would want to walk a carefully neutral path if he intended to keep his own conscience clear.

"I, uh, I reckon there ain't a whole hell of a lot of time to ponder on this, John. Not a whole hell of a lot."

"Would you let me talk to these fellows, Abner? In private. Just me and them, with Lowe not around to get their dander stirred up."

Kraus looked skeptical. "I don't know about that, John. That's askin' an awful lot, you know. I mean . . ."

"I'm not asking you to play the Judas goat, Abner. I wouldn't do that to you," Slocum assured him quietly. "I'll tell you what. You talk it over with them first. Right now if you can manage it. And if they agree to talk to me, I'll hand you my Colt and follow you to wherever they want to meet with me."

Slocum took a deep breath. He hoped he was judging Abner Kraus correctly. If not, if he was handing his gun over to a man who indeed knew that he was wanted and who might also want to turn him over to a vigilance committee . . . No, Slocum decided. He could not be judging Kraus *that* far off the mark. He had to go with his own judgment here. And if possible, he would prefer to handle the miners' complaints about and suspicions of Luke Lowe without Slocum having to gun down any of Abner Kraus's good friends. Or maybe having them gun J. Slocum down.

That was one point Slocum never allowed himself to forget. There wasn't any man born, not John Slocum nor anybody else, who couldn't be taken. Not if the boys who intended to take him had the numbers and the guts and the luck to do the job.

That was something Slocum dared *never* think. Not ever. To believe otherwise was to invite his own death through sheer tomfoolery.

"I'll ask them about it," Kraus said.

"Good. Talk to them. You know where to find me when they decide."

Abner nodded. Still looking more than a little unhappy, he turned and hurried out of the saloon.

Slocum drifted back across the room to take up

his position behind Luke Lowe. The stupid bastard, Slocum thought. He sure as hell wasn't a man worth dying for. Or killing for, either, if it came to that. But a job had been taken, and Slocum was pride- and duty-bound to carry it out as best he could. Damn it.

15

They were waiting for him in the big, ramshackle canvas and pole structure that served as the camp's only livery. There was little need here for a livery, actually. Few of the miners rode in on their own mounts, and of those who did, even fewer kept the animals once they had arrived. There simply was too little grass anywhere near Deadwood now to provide feed for the draft animals, much less for relatively useless saddle horses. At the moment the barn held a pair of Belgians, and there were a handful of mules in the pole corral behind the barn structure. Slocum could not see a single decent saddle horse in the place.

There were men enough, though. About fifteen of them, he thought with his first practiced glance. By the light of the lanterns they had hung from the support poles, he could see that the men were all rough-and-tumble miners in a broad, ragtag assortment of sizes and shapes. The only thing uniform about them was a smoldering anger that showed in their grimy, mostly unshaven faces.

At least, Slocum thought, they did not look to be badly drunk. A man just can't argue too well with a drunk, but these men who were Abner

Kraus's friends looked only lubricated, not really soused. That was something.

Slocum paused in the doorway, facing them, and sighed. Whatever happened here, he was going to catch some hell from someone. If only from that damned Luke Lowe. Slocum had caught a glimpse of the gambler's face as Slocum left his bodyguard position at the saloon to come talk to these miners. Lowe had been furious to see his protection waltz out the front door. And it had not seemed like the proper time or place for Slocum to explain to the idiot where he was going. Or that the mission was on Lowe's behalf.

The prick, Slocum thought. Given a choice, Slocum would prefer to be siding these miners, not Lowe. But he had already taken the man's money. Now he had to earn it.

"I believe you boys have some questions to ask," Slocum said as he joined them.

"Whoa up, buddy. Not so damn fast," one of the miners said.

Slocum looked the man over carefully. Whatever else this one was, he was a big son of a bitch. Taller and far heavier than Slocum's lean, long height, the miner carried huge pads of bulging muscle on his massive arms and shoulders, the kind of muscle that comes from hard work and heavy weights and lots of both. He did not look like he was any more inebriated than any of the others, but he looked somewhat angrier. Slocum recognized him as a heavy loser at the gambling table for the past two nights in a row.

"Your name is Gus, isn't it?" Slocum asked. "I think I heard you called that."

"That's right, Wilse," Gus said with his chin jutting belligerently forward. "Not that you an' me need any formal introduction. You're siding that miserable, cheating little sonuvabitch Lowe, an' that means you and me, buddy, ain't never gonna get close enough to be friends."

Slocum shrugged. "The reason I'm here, Gus, is to talk to you fellas and find out what your beef is. Keep you from an embarrassing mistake, if you know what I mean."

It was Gus who answered again. "You know an' we know that Lowe is a cheat and a cardsharp, and he's been draining off the money we grubbed out of the ground by our hard work. It's ours, by God, not some tinhorn's, and we figure to do something about a man who'd rob an honest miner."

"Bullshit," Slocum said calmly.

"What?" Gus reacted with anger, and the other men standing behind him began to stir about and look sour as well.

"You heard me right. I said bullshit, and that's what it is."

"We don't have to listen if that's all you got to say," one of the men said.

"No need for it," another grumbled.

"Calm down now, boys. That's what we're all here for, is to talk. We all agreed to that, and we all know why," Slocum said.

He stepped back a pace so he could look the group over one by one, making a point to meet each man's eyes before he shifted his gaze to the next.

"I came here," he said, "because I thought you fellas might be about to make a bad mistake and because Abner Kraus says you're good men and honest ones. He's the onliest reason I care a wad of spit what happens to any of you. Now that's a fact, boys. But if you all go off half-cocked on a bunch of wild suspicions, somebody is going to get hurt. It might be one of you, which Abner wouldn't like, or it might be Luke Lowe, who I agree is not the nicest fella around but who I owe on account of he's helped me after those Sioux got me down a while back." He grinned. "Or it might even be me. And, boys, I wouldn't like that even a little bit. Nossir. So I figured the best thing to do would be to have a talk with you and see can't we get everybody calmed down without somebody getting hurt in a damn gunfight. Why, who knows? You start shooting around one of these saloons, boys, somebody might make a *real* mistake. Some fool bastard might let off a loose shot an' kill one o' the whores." He looked very solemn and serious. "Boys, Deadwood can't afford to lose no whores."

That drew him no friendships, but at least it did make most of the men soften their expressions a little, and two of them actually chuckled some. Whores, after all, were *always* in short supply in a mining camp. Any mining camp, and particularly one as remote as this.

"The facts are the same, Wilse," Gus insisted. He had not been softened at all by Slocum's small attempt at humor. "That bastard Lowe is stealing from us. We figure to do something about it."

"I said it before, I'll say it again," Slocum told him. "Bullshit."

"I don't know where you get off saying . . ."

"Of course you do," Slocum said calmly. He kept his voice low and reserved, but the authority that used to command gray-clad troopers cut through like a finely honed steel edge and made his words carry to each of the men who faced him. "You know and I know that you are mad at Luke Lowe because he's on a lucky streak. You can't accept the idea that maybe his luck is running all that stronger than yours or that, just maybe, the man plays all that damned *smarter* than you do. But, boys, you and me both know that if you *knew,* I mean really *knew,* that the man was cheating, why, you and me wouldn't be in this here barn having a talk right now. We'd all be down at that saloon shootin' and brawlin' and riggin' a hangman's noose. 'Cause that's the way a man handles a cheat or a thief in this part of the country."

Slocum stood with his fists planted on his hips, his feet spread wide. He glared at them now, again shifting his harsh gaze from one man and on to the next, pinning them to the wall with eyes that flashed green fire and ice.

"You know that, dammit, an' so do I," he declared.

Inwardly he was wondering and hoping about how this would be received. It was a bluff, plain and simple, and it ate his guts to have to run it on these honest men when he was even surer than they that Luke Lowe was everything they said and a whole lot worse. But he had no choice. He'd taken the job. Now he had to live with it.

Prick, he again cursed Lowe in his thoughts. But he let none of that show to the men who stood in front of him.

After a moment, several of the miners' eyes fell away from his. The men began to wilt in the intensity of their anger.

No, he thought, they were not drunk. Thank goodness. They were good men and they were willing to listen to him. And, poor bastards, they were beginning to believe him. Slocum felt lousy about what he had to do.

Some of the men were beginning to back off, but not the one called Gus. Gus stepped forward, moved toward Slocum until they were eyeball to eyeball. And the big bastard had to stoop just a bit to accomplish that, Slocum saw.

"Talk about bullshit," Gus charged. "That there was some of it."

Slocum shook his head. "It wasn't and you know it, Gus. You're mad. Maybe you're broke. Lowe has what *used* to be your dust in his poke. And you're plain pissed off about it. But if you knew for a fact that Luke Lowe stole that money from you, you'd be at his throat right this minute."

"Or at yours," Gus declared. "You stand behind the man. I reckon I'd have to climb over you to get to him."

"Maybe," Slocum admitted. "I told you already, he staked me when I was down. A man has to meet his obligations. I figure you'd do the same. An' so must I."

"When it comes to it," Gus said, "an' I figure sure-God it'll come to it, Wilse, I aim to crawl your ass first then. An' I figure I can do it."

Slocum wasn't backing off an inch. Not from this man or any other. And he was beginning to get the germ of an idea.

These miners worked like hell from sunrise to sundown, digging gravel and shaking rockers and getting damn little for their efforts. A placer claim, even the best placer claim, pays small rewards for the effort that has to go into it, and at the end of a day's long toil these boys were ready for a blowout. They didn't even much care what *kind* of a blowout it might be, just so they could find one. Something to break the monotony of the work that threatened to break their backs all day every day. That was why gambling—betting on any damn thing from poker to roulette to dice to which fly was going to light first on a turd—was so damned popular in any mining camp. The fellows just plain had to have something they could look forward to.

And if they needed a diversion of some sort, one that would take their minds off of Luke Lowe and maybe go at least partway toward solving a problem Slocum seemed to be having with this Gus, who wasn't as easy to back down as the others were proving to be, why, maybe there was something Slocum could do about that.

He grinned and shoved his face nose to grubby nose with the big miner. "Gus, you done made a brag," Slocum said. "I don't think you can carry it off. I don't think there's any way in hell you are big enough or mean enough or man enough to crawl my ass. And I'm willing to bet you can't do it. I say that head to head an' one on one, I'll break your balls before you ever get close to mine, Gus. And *that's* a fact."

Slocum was more than half expecting an outburst of raw anger. Instead Gus threw back his head and howled with laughter.

"Little man," he yelped when he could get his breath again, "you done fucked up now, boy. You just challenged the best damn fighter in this whole camp. An' I figure to break your back for your trouble."

"You got to do it before you get the bragging rights to it," Slocum said.

"Then let's go at it, little man."

It had been a hell of a long time since anyone had called Slocum that. And a whole hell of a lot longer since anyone had made it stick.

"Anytime," Slocum said.

Gus balled up his massive hands into fists that Slocum saw—too late perhaps—resembled salt-cured hams more than human fists. Ropes and hawsers of thick muscle popped and curled along the man's meaty arms, and he was ready to swing. Slocum stepped back and set himself for a rush, his own fists held loose but ready. A man can wear himself out of needed arm strength just by keeping his fists clenched when he isn't swinging, and Slocum figured for this fight he might need all the endurance he could muster.

"Hold on now, dammit." It was Kraus, who had been hanging off to the sides, apparently not wanting to get into the middle of any of this discussion. Now he jumped in between the two would-be combatants. "Hold on."

"Don't get between us, Abner," Slocum protested. "This is between me and Gus. Personal."

"You bet your ass it is, little man," Gus said hotly.

"Dammit, boys, I just want you to hold up a bit here," Abner said. "If you're going to do this, you might as well do it right. We can lay out the rules. Maybe cobble a ring together. You know. Do 'er right here."

Slocum cocked his head. He laughed out loud. "Boys, I just had me an idea here. You ain't happy 'cause you're out some money. Well, my idea is this, boys. Gus and me are gonna have at it anyhow. Why don't you set up your damned ring an' invite the rest of the camp in on a payin' basis. Charge 'em at the door or something. Hell, you might get some of your money back that way. And me, I'll have the fun of whipping the shit out of old Gus here. I don't mind if it helps you fellas out some while I'm doing it."

He had them now. The group of Abner's friends began to grin and yelp. A good fight was better entertainment than most anything. Why, it even lasted longer than a good fuck. The miners crowded around the contestants, and already some were starting to lay odds and place bets.

If nothing else, Slocum thought, he had damn

sure defused their anger with Luke Lowe. They had something else to think about right now.

But he wasn't especially happy to hear how the odds were being placed. Most of the men were already having trouble finding money to go on Slocum at six to one. This Gus must be one mean son of a bitch in the ring.

16

It was morning, and John Slocum was pissed off. More to the point, he was tired of other people being pissed off at him.

The gambler was hacked because Slocum had left his backside uncovered last night, even though Slocum explained to him—several times, in increasingly vulgar terms—exactly where and why he had left the saloon.

Meg McGee was pissed with him because Slocum insisted on leaving on an errand of his own as soon as Lowe was asleep after his night's work at the tables. Meg wanted to fuck. Slocum, tired though he was, was frankly more interested in protecting his own backside. Normally he would have hated the idea of leaving a horny lady behind, unsatisfied, but at the moment there were more important things on his mind.

Protecting his own neck, keeping that good and valuable portion of his anatomy intact, took precedence over Meg McGee's moist and willing body, no matter how good she was in the sack. Slocum shut the door on her and said she could wait in his room. Maybe when he got back . . .

He left the hotel and made his way toward the cribs—mere shacks constructed of odds and ends of materials, each one looking like it was ready to fall down—that lined the gulch walls behind the row of equally flimsy saloon buildings. It was an ugly area, devoid of color or of any living, growing thing, and the whores who peered sleepily out of their curtain-hung doorways were almost as ugly.

At this time of day, with daylight barely broken, most of the women were sound asleep—or passed out cold—on the rickety cots where they plied their trade by night. The women would not be expecting much in the way of daytime customers, because the miners who provided virtually all of that trade would be working their claims every second of daylight. The miners worked even harder than they played.

Slocum picked his way slowly through the strewn garbage and broken bottles and filthy rags that littered the front of crib row. He would have to be damned hard up to want a woman from one of these places, he thought. And then he grinned at himself.

Who the hell are you trying to fool? he asked himself. There had been times enough in the past when he had been more than willing to take a crack at a woman in these conditions and worse. When a man had gone long enough without a place to put it, he'd fuck a snake if he could get somebody to hold its head, fuck a bonfire if there was a snake in it. Slocum knew. He'd been there.

A bleary-eyed old bawd stuck her head out from beneath a curtain. Her face was a mass of caked rice powder, and her lips were an indistinct smear of bright scarlet coloring. She smiled at him, and Slocum's skin crawled with the very thought of bedding her. She probably had lice at the very least, crabs and the clap almost for sure, the brain-eating French disease was possible too.

"It's only one or two, dearie," she crooned. "For a dollar I'll blow you. For two I'll blow your mind. My pussy snaps like an alligator's jaws, dearie. You won't find better along this row."

"I believe you, luv," Slocum said with a smile, "but I'm in a hurry. I need to find a girl."

"I just told you . . ."

"No, I need to find a particular girl. Me and her was on a stage together that was raided by the Sioux. Just barely got out alive together. Now I've got something of hers. I figure she'll want it. Her name's Jenny."

The old whore's face fell into disinterest. She started to turn away.

"I'll pay you for your help," Slocum said. He cursed at the necessity. He had only pocket change still, although he had been eating and drinking freely on Lowe's money since they hit town. So far the bastard had not paid him, although in truth the first week was not up yet.

"How much?" The whore turned around. She looked interested again. The professional smile— Slocum presumed it was supposed to be a smile, anyway—was back in place.

"Not much. I'm a poor man. But I'll pay you what I can."

The bawd turned blank again. She seemed to be considering her options. Finally she shrugged. Something was better than nothing, especially at this time of day.

"Jenny's in the next-to-the-last crib up that direction," she said. She hooked a thumb farther along in the direction Slocum had already been walking.

"Next to the last," he repeated.

"That's right. Now pay me, dearie."

He reached into his pocket and found a quarter, which she accepted with a grimace of disgust.

"Don't knock it," Slocum said. "Anyplace but a mining camp, that's all you'd get for a lay, old woman."

Surprisingly, she laughed. "Reckon you're right at that, sonny. An' the truth is, I've done it for less." She waved him a cheerful good-bye as he walked on toward Jenny's crib.

He shook his head. Who the hell could ever figure out a whore? Not Slocum. Nor any other man he'd ever met. They were a strange bunch, greedy and stupid for the most part. Then one would turn around and surprise you.

He stopped in front of the next-to-last crib. This Jenny was one that damn sure surprised him already. A crib girl was about the last thing in the world he would have taken her for. On the road she had bitched some, but she hadn't been foul-talking about it. He'd thought she was about as ordinary as they came.

The curtain was drawn across the sagging doorway of the tiny crib where she did her business. Slocum pushed it aside after first listening to make sure he could not hear any grunting or snorting from inside. It could be pretty unhealthy to walk in on a stranger in mid-hump.

Jennifer Porter was alone, sound asleep on the cot that occupied very nearly all of the floor space in the tiny crib. The curtain fell back across the doorway, but the sleazy material allowed enough light to penetrate that Slocum could still see. There was not much to see. A wooden box was shoved under the foot of the cot, probably holding her traveling clothes, Slocum guessed, and any personal possessions the girl might own. They had to be few if there were any at all. The box was not very large.

The floor was rock and beaten earth that had not even been shoveled flat, much less smooth. There was nothing hung on the shabby walls to relieve the ugly monotony of the crib's interior.

The girl sleeping, snoring softly, on the pole-and-rope cot was the same girl Slocum remembered from the week before, but now she was wearing a thin chemise that covered her only to mid-thigh. Her hair was unpinned now and flowing loose across the burlap sack, probably stuffed with straw, that served her for a pillow.

She seemed very small in her sleep, unhealthily thin. Her skin was pale and grainy in texture, completely unlike the satin smoothness that Meg McGee offered for Slocum's use. At least she seemed to make some effort to keep herself clean. He could see a line of grime—all of Deadwood seemed to be a collection of dirt and dust looking for a place to light—at the back and sides of her neck where she must have washed her face but missed some of the omnipresent filth she lived in.

She looked, Slocum thought, very vulnerable in her sleep. For a moment he wondered what might have brought a girl like this into the trade, but he knew he would never ask her. A whore just naturally will lie to that often-asked question, and it is only a mug who will ask it in the first place.

One long step carried Slocum the entire length of the miserable little crib, and he reached down to shake the girl awake.

"Huh? Wha?" She sat up in confusion, looking wildly about. Slocum thought he could see stark terror reflecting in enlarged eyes, but she quickly recognized him and calmed down. "It's you. Hi."

"Hi yourself." He pulled a cigar from his shirt

pocket and bit off the twist. He took his time about lighting it.

"You, uh, come here for a fuck, did you?" she asked.

He shook his head and exhaled a cloud of thick, fine-tasting smoke.

"I didn't think so." She did not sound disappointed. The girl swung her legs off the cot so she was perched on the side of the bed and slid to the far end of it. "Sit down if you like."

"Thanks." Slocum sat, carefully gauging the distance between them so that it was not so great that she would take offense nor so near that she might think he was interested in her skinny body. She sounded, and now she looked, much older than he had pegged her for back on the road. "How are you getting along?"

Jenny shrugged. "I make a living. In its own way, it's an honest living. Is that anything to you?" Briefly, there was a flash of something in her eyes. It might have been pride, Slocum thought. If he was correct, that was an odd thing to see there.

"I didn't come here to preach to you, if that's what you're thinking. And I didn't come here to abuse you. We shared a rough experience a little while back. That's all."

"That isn't why you came here, though," she observed.

She was not entirely stupid, Slocum thought. And her language was not the gutter slur or the vulgarity one might expect from a crib whore. The girl was a puzzlement indeed.

"No, I didn't," he admitted. "I came to ask a favor of you."

The curiosity that was in her expression snapped closed, and she give him a guarded, wary look. Favors were something all whores knew about. Sometimes they were harmless. Sometimes expensive. Sometimes painful if not actually fatal.

"I won't make any promises until I hear what you're asking," she said.

"I wouldn't expect you to. It's a small thing," he said. "A correction, really. Apparently, while we were on the road that time, you misheard my name. I just wanted to correct that impression. That's all."

The girl's eyebrows hiked up.

"My name is Wilse," Slocum said. He looked her straight in the eyes. "The name you thought was mine belongs to a man who's wanted here and there. Probably not in Deadwood. But a man never knows."

"I see." Intelligence showed in the hazel eyes she fixed on him. He was sure she did understand. "I owe you already for the help you gave me back there, Mr. Wilse. I would not want to inadvertently do anything that might hurt you now."

Slocum smiled at her. "I appreciate that, Miss Porter. If ever I can do you a favor, I would be happy to. And I do mean that. Anything I can do, I gladly will."

"I believe you do mean it, Mr. Wilse," she said slowly. Now it seemed to be her turn to be surprised. "And I thank you. For that and for . . . calling me Miss Porter when you obviously know better."

Slocum smiled and shook his head. "No, I think it is the proper term to use."

For a moment Slocum thought he could see a hint of moisture welling up in the girl's eyes, but a whore doesn't cry. She blinked rapidly and shook her head.

She looked away. When she glanced toward Slocum again she had herself under control. She gave him a casual, even a friendly smile. "I hear you are fighting big Gus Kane tonight."

"So it seems," Slocum said.

"The odds are all on Gus, you know."

"I know," Slocum said with a grin, "and I sure wish I had some money to lay on myself."

"Surely you don't think you can take him." She sounded genuinely startled. "He has beaten every man in this camp who dared to try him." She laughed. "I think he has told that to every . . . girl . . . along this entire row. At least three times apiece."

"I've heard that too," Slocum said easily. He smiled and stood up. "But the truth is, Miss Porter, I figure to win. You see, I don't fight fair."

She laughed and said, "Maybe I should put my money on you then, Mr. Wilse. The last odds I heard before daylight they were offering twelve to one."

"Yup. Sure wish I had a few dollars in my poke to put up. Those odds would be enough to get a man out of this dump."

The girl looked thoughtful. "Or a girl," she said wistfully.

"Or a girl," Slocum agreed. "If she wanted out."

"I . . ." She shook her head. "Never mind. Sometimes I think with my mouth. That is a very bad habit to get into, Mr. Wilse. Believe me. I know."

The girl gave him a bright and apparently very genuine smile. She stood and offered a small hand, which he took, and with all the gallantry, however long unused, of an officer and a gentleman of the Confederacy, John Slocum, onetime captain of cavalry, made a graceful leg and bowed low over the almost naked little whore's hand. Lightly he brushed the backs of her fingers with his lips before he straightened.

"Good day, Miss Porter. Good fortune." Slocum turned and swept out through the flimsy curtain over the crib doorway. In the morning sunlight Slocum felt taller and stronger and, somehow, *better* than he had felt in a very long time.

17

The ring was not particularly to Slocum's liking, but then the conditions would be as poor for Gus as they were for him. There was not a building in Deadwood big enough to hold the crowd that had gathered for this diversion, so Abner's friends had put this excuse for a prize ring in the middle of a corral with gravel and mule shit for a floor.

Four stakes had been driven into the hard earth with a single rope run along the top of the stakes to form the ring itself. It was enough to tell the crowd where to stop pushing forward but not much better than that. And no one had bothered to pad the splintered wooden posts that formed the corners. The area was about twenty feet square, possibly less.

The light was lousy too. No one in his right mind would schedule any kind of event during daylight hours in a mining camp, and this fight was no exception. It was long since dark now, and the night was barely softened by a group of torches and hastily assembled lanterns and lamps set on the original corral posts that surrounded the makeshift ring. The lights were too weak and too far away to completely dispel the gloom of the night. But, again, the conditions would be no better for Gus than for Slocum. The men had done the best they could under the circumstances, and Slocum was not complaining.

The audience—hell, they must have drawn every man and boy from the entire Black Hills discovery —had already overflowed the corral and were perched on top of every shack, pole, and rooftop in sight. If even a quarter of them paid to watch, Slocum thought, Abner and his friends were going to do mighty well for themselves.

Slocum cursed his own stupidity at not demanding a share of the take, but he just hadn't thought of it at the time. And worse yet, he still had no money to bet on himself except for a single, lousy dollar that he had been able to scrape together. He had placed that with a bartender at Lowe's favorite saloon at fifteen to one. He would feel at least a little bit better, though, if he could get that $15 in his jeans. And tomorrow he should get another $50 from Lowe. It still would not be enough to get him out of here, he knew, but it would be a start. He was looking forward to that, for the moment looking past the coming fight with big Gus. After all, he really did not intend to fight fair.

Slocum looked over his shoulder. That bastard Lowe was there in Slocum's corner, all right, but Slocum guessed that was only so the prick could stay close enough to holler for help from Slocum if he got into trouble himself. The man had bitched a blue streak when he found out about the fight, but by then it was too late. Besides, there would be no poker playing going on anywhere in Deadwood until the match was ended. Lowe had little choice about delaying his crooked play.

Slocum grinned to himself. Lowe had never once asked Slocum if he thought he could take Gus, and Lowe had heard all the tales that Slocum had about Gus's prowess as a fighter. Slocum suspected that Luke Lowe was laying his money on Gus.

That was fine by J. Slocum. As far as he was concerned, Lowe was entitled to take a real bath on this fight. In fact, Slocum hoped he did, and that the miners would clean Lowe out. Except, of course, for the $50 he owed the lean, hard outlaw. Piss on the man.

Slocum was ready, stripped to his boots and jeans, with his shirt and metal-buckled belt removed in readiness for the combat. It was to be a bare-knuckle affair under slightly modified prize-fighting rules. Anything a man could do to his opponent while standing on his feet was fair. A knockdown ended the round, and there was a one-minute rest between rounds. The fight would end when one of the contestants was unable to toe the scratch when time was called for the next round. Very simple.

A sound not unlike a pack of wolves at full bay went up from the audience, and Slocum could see Gus and his retinue of friends and admirers pushing a path through the mob. Damn near the whole crowd went wild with frenzy as their man ducked under the rope and came hopping and leaping into the center of the ring with his arms upraised like he had already won the damn fight.

If nothing else, Slocum admitted, he had sure won the crowd. And damned if he didn't look like he was ready to meet the obligations of his reputation, too. Like Slocum, he was already stripped to jeans and boots, and with his shirt off, he looked a good three times the size and strength of Slocum's wiry body.

Slocum would have expected a man that size to look like a grizzly bear, but instead his upper body was almost hairless. It was not, though, without muscle. Slocum had seen twisted steel cables that looked weaker than Gus's muscles. And they were piled pretty deep, too.

Gus looked across the ring and thumbed his nose at Slocum.

"Fuck you," Slocum returned cheerfully.

The crowd roared anew, and a puny little fellow who looked like he was in the last stages of the consumption reached across the rope to pat Slocum's shoulder. "Make me some money, mister," he said.

"The odds were just too good to resist, huh?" Slocum asked.

The fellow grinned happily. "How else could them other boys get any takers?"

Slocum shook his head. So much for his faithful followers. Shee-it!

Abner Kraus stepped into the center of the ring between the two fighters, and the crowd grew quiet. As a friend of both men, Abner was the only one any of the crowd would have agreed to trust as referee. Abner held up his hands, and the last sounds died down around them.

"We all know why we're here, boys," Abner shouted. "We all know the rules, such as they be. There's no point in assin' around out here. May the best man *win*." Abner pointed a finger at a fellow seated on a stool at ringside, and the other miner clanged an upended stew pot with a hammer. The dull gong could be clearly heard on the chilly night air, and Gus began to bounce forward, moving lightly on his toes and already beginning to stalk his much lighter opponent.

Shee-it, Slocum thought. He looks big as a fucking locomotive. But if you can't run, boy, you'd best win. Slocum hunched his chin down toward his chest and began to shuffle forward with an ungainly, flat-footed stance.

Gus, watching him move, grinned broadly and turned his head to posture for a moment before his admirers. "Pour me a beer, Charlie," he called. "This ain't gonna take long at all."

While Gus was so engaged in self-admiration, Slocum dropped his pretense of awkwardness and darted forward. His right hand lashed out like a cracking whip, not fisted but with the knuckles of his first finger joints thrust forward like a knife blade.

The lethal plane of solid knuckle sliced into Gus's throat, and the big man went off his feet like a poleaxed steer at the slaughterhouse.

But dammit, Slocum saw, the man's head had been turned, and most of the fearsome blow had been taken on the slab of hard muscle on the side of Gus's neck. A solid shot to the Adam's apple would have ended the fight then and there, but Slocum had not been that lucky.

Nor was he likely to get a second chance now.

Still, the first round was ended. Slocum walked calmly back to his corner and stood waiting while Gus laboriously crawled to his own corner and climbed the post to regain his feet.

It was, Slocum thought, like watching a felled tree rise again.

Jesus, but the man looked huge.

And mad. Lordy, but he did look mad.

All of a sudden this wasn't a diversion anymore. From now on, Gus was going to be serious about this business.

Slocum stood and patiently waited for the time-keeper to bash his gong for the second round.

18

Slocum shook his head, wagging it from side to side like a mortally wounded buffalo bull. He winced. Maybe that description wasn't so far off the mark. Too damn close to be accurate, that was for sure. Blood ran down the side of his face and flew off the point of his jaw with every motion of his aching head.

He could hear a distant ringing in his ears. Or in the places where he used to have ears. He was not entirely sure they were still in place.

Jesus, he thought, that couldn't be the start of the next round already.

No, he was down on one knee. He was sure—pretty sure, anyhow—that he had just gone down. This time. Again. He was not real positive how many times that had happened so far. Several, anyway. Shee-it. He shook his head again and ran an already bloody forearm across his forehead. That wiped some of the blood away, and he could see somewhat better. An improvement. A definite improvement.

Damn but this Gus could fight.

Slocum came to his feet and staggered back to his corner. He leaned on the wooden post that used to support the ring rope. The rope was long since gone. Slocum had gone flying out through it often enough by now that only one side of the marked ring remained intact.

He took several deep gulps of badly needed air. He was quivering with fatigue, and when he turned around to peer across the trampled arena that was their ring he could see Gus standing quietly in his opposing corner, still looking strong.

Not fresh, exactly. Slocum was no slouch when it came to fighting, and if he did stay down he wasn't going to leave Gus a virgin. The man had taken punishment too. Slocum at least could claim that.

Slocum bent over and opened his mouth wide. He drew healing oxygen deep into his lungs, held it, and let it out slowly. He felt better. He might even—he hoped—be collecting his second wind.

At least he wasn't feeling much pain now. A welcome numbness had set into the battered portions of his head and body, and the pain he had been feeling was no longer anywhere near as intense as it had been.

Deliberately, he looked across at Gus. And grinned.

Gus did not respond with a taunt of his own. The man looked weary, by God. And Slocum felt encouraged. Maybe ol' Gus was worse off than he had thought. Slocum grinned again.

That damned wimp with the stew pot beat on the metal again. *Why couldn't the little creep get distracted for a minute or two?* The round, whichever one it was, was under way.

Slocum shuffled forward. His flat-footed stance was no come-on trick this time. He just wasn't fresh enough to bounce on his toes now. But then neither was Gus. They both moved like a couple of tired old men.

Gus waded in and started a roundhouse right that came sweeping in from somewhere over in the next section and whistled powerfully, if slowly, over Slocum's ducking head.

Since he happened to be down there anyway in the process of ducking that looping right, Slocum pounded a few short, straight jabs into Gus's ribs and breadbasket. It felt like he was hitting a side of hanging beef, but he could hear the air whistling out of Gus's overworked lungs.

Both men, as if by some unspoken cue, backed away from each other and stood for a moment with their heads hanging, staring at each other and grabbing immense gulps of air into their lungs.

Slocum raised his head and forced his aching body erect. He let his arms dangle, resting them for the few seconds he might have before Gus shuffled forward yet again, as he had been doing repeatedly, doggedly, ever since the fight began.

At this point Slocum was going on pride alone. But, by damn, he had a-plenty of that. He motioned Gus toward him.

They closed again. Shambling. Stumbling. Conscious of nothing but each other. The crowd was going madly wild around them, but neither man knew or heard or cared. All they could see was each other.

Slocum would have been pleased to know that now there were a fair number of miners in the audience who were waving their pokes of gold dust in the air and inviting those same long odds that had been offered against Slocum before the fight. But now there were no takers. Now the odds were down to four to one and going begging at that rate.

Gus moved in again. Again he tried that sweeping right that Slocum and everyone else could see coming a good two seconds before it ever started. Gus did not seem to know or to care how badly he was telegraphing that vainly hopeful punch. He seemed only to want to connect with it, just once, and tear Slocum's head off so Gus could quit the ring and get some rest.

Once again Slocum ducked and beat a rapid-fire tattoo on Gus's ribs. The bigger man faltered. His guarding left hand fell toward his waist. He was tired. Perhaps even more so than John Slocum. He wanted to rest.

He got his wish.

Slocum shifted to his right, past the fallen guard, and laid his entire weight into a long right lead that, from some reserve Slocum had not really been sure he still possessed, managed to find some snap and zing.

Gus's head snapped back at the impact, and his eyes rolled. He stumbled backward, caught himself, and overcorrected, going down hard on his knees.

"Time!" Abner screamed. Kraus jumped in between the two and turned Slocum by the shoulders, pointing him toward his corner to make sure he knew the round was over.

Slocum made his way stiff-legged back to his corner.

The place was his corner by location but not by assistance. He had not seen Lowe there for some time, and no one else seemed interested in helping him, in swabbing his face with a damp cloth or offering him a beer to rinse the dust and incredible dryness from his throat. He stood there alone and untended, but he stood there unbeaten.

Pride, he told himself. Balls. Stand up. Throw your head back. Drink that cool night air and let

them know you're a man. If you do go out, by
God, make 'em carry you, because you'll be too
whipped to crawl. If you can crawl you can stand,
and if you can stand you can fight. And, an inner
voice demanded of him, if you can fight you can
win. Do it.

He turned.

The cretin with the stew pot bashed it again,
and Slocum stood where he was, waiting for Gus
to cross the ring to him.

Gus was far gone now. Very far gone. He staggered like a man on the tail end of a nine-day
drunk as he waded forward on rubber knees.

The big man drew back his right fist again, and
Slocum kept a wary, blood-clouded eye on that
massive fist. If it ever once connected, all Slocum's efforts could be for naught.

Instead, this time, Gus's left jabbed forward. It
caught Slocum on the side of his jaw, and he could
hear those bells again.

He allowed his head to roll with the punch, ab-
sorbing some of the power of that straight left,
and the impact spun him partially around.

Gus, sensing a kill, gathered his last remaining
vestiges of strength and jumped forward with a
flurry of pummeling rights and lefts.

Overwhelmed by the windmill attack, Slocum
dodged aside, feinting a lunge forward and then
leaping back, somehow managing to keep his feet
on legs that no longer wanted to support him.

The big miner, punching like an automaton,
seemed unaware for a moment that his target was
no longer before him. Gus continued to flail the
air where Slocum had been, and Slocum took the
opportunity to sidestep.

Slocum slid to the side and sent another solid

right crashing against the edge of Gus's jaw. The big man's legs wobbled.

Good, Slocum thought. Now. Shifting his weight to his left leg, he lashed out with his right boot, catching Gus on the side of his already wobbly knee.

Gus's leg buckled, and the miner sprawled forward.

They were still cramped into Slocum's corner, and Gus lurched headfirst into the unpadded wood of the fence post. The solid wood caught him across the forehead in a blow more powerful than Slocum was capable of delivering at that point.

Gus tumbled down onto his side and flopped onto his back with his eyes rolled back in his head, vacant, bloodshot whites showing between slitted eyelids.

Slocum staggered. He grabbed a spectator's shoulder for support. He did not dare fall now.

He stood panting and gasping, waiting. Where was the damned gong? Why wasn't that little weasel with the gong doing his job? Why had he chosen *this* round to go take a piss?

It didn't matter. Not any longer. This time Gus was not going to get up again for quite a while.

Eventually, it seemed like an eternity or possibly an hour or two longer than that, Slocum heard the sound of the hammer striking the pot. It seemed to come from a very long ways off.

He coughed and spat. There was no saliva left in his mouth, only blood from the numerous cuts inside his cheeks. The blood made a dusty, black lump in the dirt of the corral floor.

But it didn't matter. Nothing mattered now.

He could hear, from that same great distance away, the sounds of men roaring their excitement and approval and, some of them, anger.

The hell with them. The hell with everything. He didn't have to keep his feet any longer.

John Slocum collapsed into the trampled mule manure they had been fighting in. Both men had to be carried away from the ring.

19

Slocum was a mass of aches and bruises. He could hardly tell where one hurt began and another left off. Nor was he entirely sure where he was right now except that he was not in his own bed back at the hotel.

He tried to open his eyes and gave it up for the time being after a brief, painful struggle. Both eyes were swelled shut and glued together by the pus or whatever it was that had been weeping out of them during the night.

He tried to remember back to the night before, following the fight. He remembered being carried into a saloon where someone poured beer over his head and someone else—probably one of the few who had been tantalized enough by the odds to have placed some money on him—poured beer into his throat. That, he remembered, had been about as good as anything was ever likely to taste to him if he lived for a hundred years. Which, the way he felt right now, was not real likely.

There had been a number of other beers offered and then some whiskey and after that . . . he couldn't remember. What with one thing and another it had all run together in his brain like some sort of homogenous glop, and now the rest of the night was was lost to him. Including wherever it was he was waking up.

Slocum stirred and felt of the bed he was lying on. His sense of touch told him little except that the bed was a small one and the mattress was lumpy. He was covered by a rough-textured blanket, and there seemed to be no sheets on the bed. The hotel supplied sheets. Slocum had no idea where he might have ended up.

Or with whom. He heard someone else moving nearby.

For an instant there was a flash of near-panic in his mind as he found himself defenseless and virtually blind, but almost as quickly he heard a woman's voice.

"Lie still, and don't try to open your eyes. I'll bathe them open for you. It's all right. You will be fine here, Mr. Wilse."

The voice sounded vaguely familiar and its tone was soothing. He felt the light brush of a soft hand across his forehead, and the woman said, "I'll be right back with some water. It will be all right now."

There was a crunching sound of light footsteps that quickly faded, and Slocum could sense that he was alone. He tried again to open his swollen, pain-filled eyes, but the results were no better than they had been before. He lay back and gave it up. She, whoever she was, had said she would be right back. If he heard any other, heavier tread, *then* he could worry. In the meantime he would do as she had suggested.

She was back a minute or two later, and he could hear water sloshing in a basin. He felt the weight of a small body taking a seat on the edge of the bed beside him, and a moment later he felt the refreshing, cooling touch of a wet cloth being gently patted over his eyes.

"This should do the trick," she said. She laughed softly. "I've done this often enough before. For my brothers."

The woman's touch—he was sure it was not Meg McGee now but could not for the life of him remember who it might be—was both gentle and competent. "Try to open them now," she said. "Slowly. Just a bit at a time now."

He did. Her ministrations had done the intended work, and this time his eyes popped open after little effort.

"Jenni . . . Miss Porter," he said.

She laughed. "You didn't know?"

Slocum shook his head. He grinned. "I couldn't remember. Sorry."

"I am not surprised, actually. You were not in very good condition when you dragged in here this morning."

"Did I . . . ?"

"If you are asking if you disgraced yourself," she smiled, "I think the answer would have to be yes. And no."

"What . . . ?"

"The yes part is that you were quite rude to a gentleman caller, well, a customer of mine who happened already to be here. Threw the poor fellow out, actually. The no part is that once you were comfortably installed on my cot, you were no further bother, save for some rather loud snoring. At least you made no demands. And you *did* address me as Miss Porter, even in that condition." Her smile became broader. "So what could I do but allow you to remain?"

"Oh, Jeez. I am sorry." He tried to sit up and after a struggle managed it.

"It is all right. Really. And I do owe you quite a lot, Mr. Wilse."

"For that business a week ago? Forget it. You've more than made up for any little thing I might have done then. After all, it was my own neck I was looking out for. You just happened to be in the same general neighborhood."

"No," she said, "not for that at all." She chuckled. Damned if she didn't sound younger than he remembered, Slocum thought.

"I took your advice, Mr. Wilse," she went on.

"Advice?" He couldn't remember having given her any.

"About the fight last night. There was a great deal of wagering going on, you know. And I did have a little money laid by after a week on the row."

Slocum looked at her. He thought she was beginning to weep a little now, although he couldn't understand why that might be.

"You told me you would win," she continued. "I believed you. I put a hundred fifty dollars down at sixteen to one, Mr. Wilse." She definitely was crying now. "So you see, Mr. Wilse, you have earned me quite a lot of money. Enough . . ."

"Are you all right?" She seemed unable to speak anymore Her shoulders were racked with the heavy, soul-deep sobbing that comes from only the deepest and most painful emotions. "Miss Porter, are you all right?"

She nodded her head and used the hem of her short chemise to wipe her eyes. "Yes. I'm . . . fine. Really. Thanks to you. Really."

Slocum reached out to pet her shoulder and smooth the hair hanging loose down her back.

After a moment she looked at him and gave him

a tear-streaked smile. "I . . . suppose I owe you an explanation."

"No, you don't owe me a thing, Miss Porter. Not a thing."

"Thank you, but . . . Perhaps you are right. Perhaps I just . . . want to talk about it."

"I'm a good listener," he said.

She nodded. The flow of tears was subsiding. "I am . . . a whore, Mr. Wilse. Mr. . . . . Slocum. If you will permit me that. I promise you I will not mention it to anyone else."

"Of course."

"Yes, well, as I was saying, I am a whore. A soiled dove, some might call it. A crib girl. The lowest form of human existence."

"But . . ."

"No. Please don't interrupt. It is the simple truth, Mr. Slocum Neither you nor I can deny it; it just is. But I have not always been . . . what I am."

"That's pretty plain, Miss Porter. The way you talk, the way you hold yourself. Nobody could mistake that about you."

"Thank you." She smiled for the first time since the tears had begun. "I seem to be constantly having to thank you for one reason or another, don't I? Never mind, though. And I won't go into all the shabby details. They would only bore you in any event."

He started to protest again, but she cut him off with a small hand raised to his lips.

"I come from a decent, God-fearing family, Mr. Slocum. I was raised to be like them. But like so many other innocents, I fell in love with the wrong man. And . . ." She shook her head. "No boring details. I did promise. Suffice it to say that I ended up here, with no respect for myself, not an ounce

more than my customers had for me. But I think
you have changed that, Mr. Slocum. It is that that
I am deeply, truly grateful to you for. That more
than anything else in the world you could possibly
have done for me. And now, with the winnings
you—again you—brought to me, Mr. Slocum, I
think . . . I think I am strong enough now, determined enough, that I can take my winnings and
board a stagecoach away from this place. I think
. . . I can go . . . somewhere. I don't know where. I
really don't much care where it will be Somewhere
in the East possibly. Somewhere where cribs and
fifty-cent whores are an idea foreign to them. I
will have enough money, thanks to you, to establish a little business for myself. As a dressmaker,
possibly. I used to be quite good with a needle and
thread. And I have sense of style and taste—
enough I think to get by. I don't require a great
deal, you see. A small business in a small town
would suit me very happily."

She smiled. "I guess I sound like every whore
who has ever lived. But I really do intend to try it.
I intend to give it my very best."

Slocum petted her again. "I'm willing to bet you
make it stick too, Miss Porter. I'd sure bet on that."

20

Slocum awakened the second time feeling not good but a hell of a lot better. Judging from the failing light seeping through the closed crib curtain he guessed it was getting on toward evening, and he would soon have to go find Lowe. There was still the money that was owed him. Plus the winnings, small though they were, that the barkeep owed him. Things were definitely looking up, he thought.

He sat up, this time without help, and looked around. Jennifer Porter was perched on a small stool in the narrow aisle between the cot and the wall of her crib. She smiled when she saw him look her way.

"Welcome back," she said.

"I am sure do feel better. But hey, I've been flopped out in your bed all day long and I guess most of the night, too. What about you, Miss Porter?"

"I have no need for it any longer. And I suppose I shall have to readjust to the idea of working by day and sleeping by night, anyway. You merely gave me a head start on that."

Slocum grinned. "Good. That means you haven't changed your mind. I'm real pleased for you."

"You really are, aren't you."

142

"Yeah, I reckon I really am."

"Mr. Slocum, could I ask you . . . one favor? If you wouldn't be offended, that is?"

"You can ask me anything. Likely I'll even agree, though I can't guarantee it."

The light was growing poor, but Slocum could have sworn he saw the girl blush before she spoke again. "There is one thing . . . but you don't have to do it if you don't want."

"You already said that."

"Yes, well . . . When I find this place where I will stay and try to make a home for myself, wherever that is, I do not think I will be interested in . . . male companionship. If you know what I mean."

"I can understand that, I think. You likely got a pretty low opinion of the breed. Sometimes I do too, though for a different reason than you."

She nodded. "Something like that. And other reasons as well. Which is not important, really. But what I wanted to ask . . . John . . ." She looked up, seeking his approval.

"Yes?"

"What I had in mind, one last time, with a man . . . well, I think you are wonderfully strong, John. But I believe you can be a gentle man as well." She smiled faintly. "Yesterday, when you kissed my hand . . . I haven't felt that grand in years. Perhaps never before. And I wondered . . . would you find it offensive to . . . to take me to bed, John?"

She was not looking at him now, and she sounded very timid, as if she feared his rejection, as if that might be a blow to her that would destroy all the gains in self-esteem she had made in the past day or two. There was no way Slocum could have refused her request. Not when he, in his own way and for his own reasons, owed Jennifer Porter so very much.

"I would be honored, Miss Porter." He reached out and touched her hand softly. "Jennifer."

She rose and stood before him. With one slow, fluid motion that could only have come from frequent practice, she stripped her chemise over her head and stood before him. But suddenly her courage and her crib girl's easy familiarity with the ways and the desires of the male animal deserted her, and she turned her face shyly away from him, standing with her small hands futilely covering her tiny, rosebud breasts and skimpy patch of brown pubic hair like a wood nymph in a classical painting.

"You are lovely," Slocum said in a voice scarcely more than a whisper.

Slowly, with great tenderness, he placed his fingertips to her side and gently traced the indentation to her slim waist and the soft swell of her finely shaped hip and flank. He could feel her tremble at his touch.

Carefully, feeling that he was the bearer of a heavy responsibility, the outlaw John Slocum drew the girl to him and down onto the bed at his side.

He covered her face—not nearly so plain in his eyes now as she once had seemed—with kisses as light as the touch of down floating on summer air.

The girl's eyes remained closed, but he could feel her slender body begin to stir beneath his touch, and when he kissed her lips, they opened as she responded to him. She sighed and moved to accommodate him, raising herself onto the cot at his side and pressing herself against him.

For a long time they lay in that embrace, kissing and touching, the girl gradually becoming more emboldened as Slocum's desires rose.

She broke away from him after a time and, with a smile far sweeter than any crib girl could have been capable of giving, bent over him and began to remove his clothing.

Jennifer pressed Slocum's shoulders back against the rough ticking that covered the straw of her mattress and began to cover his neck and battered, purple-splotched torso with a rain of quick, light kisses.

She licked his nipples with a darting, practiced tongue and captured snatches of hair from his chest between her lips, tugging at them playfully and obviously enjoying what she was doing to and for him.

Oddly, after the days he had spent romping with the gorgeous Meg, Slocum began to be more aroused now than he had been since that last morning with Marlene Brooke, and his erection was a demanding, throbbing animal with an insistence that could not be denied.

She moved lower, running her talented tongue around the rim of his navel and dipping into it again and again in a strange parody of a male entering a woman, although now it was she who was entering him.

Slocum moaned. He could not help himself, and the intensity of what he was feeling with this skinny little whore was disturbing. Frequently flip and irreverent when he found himself in an emotional situation, he just barely remembered in time to avoid telling her that she was a talent too great not to be professional. That, he knew, would have destroyed for the girl everything that she had gained, and to have said it would have been inexcusable. He sighed.

Jennifer moved lower still, and she drew him

into the warm depths of her throat slowly and with a deep tenderness that added to the physical part of what she was giving him.

The girl was not just serving him. She was giving to him. Completely giving. And she seemed to be taking more pleasure from that act of giving than Meg McGee was capable of receiving from her wildest, most explosive climaxes.

Slocum reached down and lightly stroked the girl's head while she ministered to his pleasure, and he felt a warmth toward her that he never would have suspected might be remotely possible.

With a sigh she left him and lay at his side, pressing her small body against his lean, muscular frame.

"John. Please?"

Slocum smiled. "Gladly, Jennifer Porter. More gladly than you will ever guess."

He took her then, but this was no wild coupling, no ramming together of flesh with flesh. What she was giving him was more than a race toward the explosion of sperm into woman-flesh. Their joining was more of a rite than a fuck, and each seemed to know it.

They moved slowly together, she rising to meet him and then the two drawing softly apart, and in this too she was completely giving and patient so that Slocum never suspected she was building with her own passions beneath his hard body. It came as a complete surprise to him when the girl shuddered and bit her underlip and quietly convulsed under his moving hips.

He looked into her face, and her eyes were wide with incredulity. She began first to smile and then to cry, and she shook her head abruptly from side to side.

"Never," she whispered. "Never. I never knew it could be like this. This was . . . beautiful, John. It was truly beautiful."

She began to sob harder and buried her small face in the hollow of his throat.

"Thank you . . . thank you . . . thank you," she repeated over and over.

It was minutes later before she realized that he had not yet come, and with a look of joy she began expertly to pump her hips against him. With pleasure she built him high and higher and ever higher until Slocum believed he could take no more, the pleasure so intense it bordered on pain, and only then did she fling him over the edge of the precipice where she had been holding him. Only then did she bring him to a shattering, shuddering climax that was so intense he cried out aloud in the darkness of the tiny crib.

They parted their bodies without words—there were no words they could have used to each other at that moment—and separately began to dress, he in the only clothing he owned and she in the traveling gown she had been wearing when Slocum first saw her back on the long, dusty stage road to Cheyenne.

Only when they were both dressed and he was ready to leave did Jennifer speak to him again.

"I will be leaving on the northbound stage tomorrow morning," she said. "I don't expect to see you again. That probably is for the best. I don't know that I could bear to leave Deadwood if I were to see you again. I . . . I truly did not know that a man and a woman together could . . . have so much. It was never like that for me before, and it may never be like that again. But . . . you have given me that, John Slocum. In addition to all the rest, you have given me that. And I think I thank you more for that gift than for any of the others."

He thought she was crying, but it was too dark now to tell. Jennifer took an elegant-looking gold beaded handbag from beneath her cot—from beneath what *had been* her cot—and clutched it in trembling hands. "While you were sleeping this afternoon I collected my wager. My future. That, like all the rest, is your doing, John Slocum. If I can . . ."

"Don't go insulting me now, Miss Porter. Don't go making any offers that I'd get mad about." He laid his hands over hers and could feel the large, satisfying bulge the wad of currency made inside the bag she was holding.

"I didn't think you would, but . . ."

In a flash of understanding Slocum realized something, and for a moment it almost made him angry with her. "Tell me something," he demanded. "Just now, that was a gift, wasn't it, and not a need? Wasn't it?"

She looked down away from him and nodded almost imperceptibly. "At first it was," she admitted in a small voice. "It was supposed to be like that." She looked up. "But it didn't turn out that way, John. Please believe me. It seems that I told you the truth to begin with even though I had no idea at the time that it was true. I just . . ." Her voice broke. "Please, John. Before I decide I can't go. Please leave me now. And . . . think about me . . . from time to time."

Slocum smiled. "As a fine and lovely lady who is a dressmaker. Yes, Jennifer. I will think about you." He rose for the last time and turned, but instead of kissing her good-bye, he once again bowed to her with a graceful leg and lightly touched his lips to the backs of her fingers.

"Good fortune, Miss Porter. Good-bye."

He turned and got the hell out of there before he turned completely soft in his old age.

But he did feel mighty good as he walked away from the crib.

21

"You're late!"

Slocum bristled at the snappish tone Lowe had used and his eyes flashed green fire at the gambler. Slocum was still sore and aching, and that was Lowe's fault. He did not intend to take any crap off the man tonight.

"I should have been at the table an hour ago," Lowe persisted grumpily, but after seeing the look on Slocum's face he was not speaking nearly as harshly now as he had a moment earlier.

"Bullshit," Slocum said mildly. "There's never any marks worth fleecing this early in the evening. Besides," he added with an evil grin, "you should of made enough money off me in that fight last night to make up for a couple weeks away from the table."

"Huh!" Lowe snapped. But he said nothing more.

Meaning, Slocum decided, that the man had bet on Gus, just like Slocum expected he would, and had lost his damn shirt. Good.

"Speaking of money," Slocum said, "I've been watching your backside for a week now. The way I remember it that means I'm entitled to fifty dollars."

Lowe gave him no argument on the subject but reached into his coat and pulled out a wallet that was fat with paper currency. The bastard hadn't been cleaned then, Slocum thought. Pity.

The gambler peeled off a pair of twenties and a ten and handed them to Slocum. "Unless you'd rather have hard money," he said.

Slocum shrugged. "This will spend just as good." He took the bills and jammed them deep into his jeans.

Come to think of it, he realized, Luke Lowe always paid for everything in currency or, occasionally, in coin, yet it was mostly placer dust that he took in from his poker games. Slocum wondered idly where all that bright, beautiful, flaky yellow stuff was going to. By now Lowe must have quite a pile of it set aside.

It was impossible for Slocum to avoid wondering if he should relieve Mr. Lowe of the responsibility of caring for all that pretty stuff. But dammit, he *was* taking the man's money to guard him—presumably therefore the gold as well. Dammit. And to think that Luke Lowe was such a bastard. It would have been a pleasure for Slocum to whop him over the head and make off with Lowe's profits, leaving the prick alive afterward to know who had taken it.

Slocum sighed. It just wasn't in him. Not with Lowe's cash in his pocket and with a week's obligation to the bastard for every mouthful of food and sip of drink that had gone down Slocum's gullet. Sure was a pity, though. He turned and followed the gambler out into the hotel hallway and down the stairs toward the street and the saloon where they would spend most of the night.

The early evening—and in spite of Lowe's complaints they had arrived well before most of the gamblers—passed routinely enough, and Slocum's biggest problem of the night looked to be the usual one of staying awake through it all.

He looked for Abner Kraus, but neither he nor any of his friends that Slocum could have recognized showed up, which Slocum thought odd. Still, the night was not a total loss. Slocum collected his winnings, meager though they were, from the bartender and felt much better with some money in his pockets for a change.

Another week, he figured, and he could get the hell out of Deadwood and leave Luke Lowe behind. That in itself was a pleasurable enough thought to take the edge off his boredom.

It was very late, along toward the shank of the night, when the crowd of miners was beginning to clear out in favor of an hour or two of sleep before their next workday began, when Abner finally made an appearance.

At least, Slocum saw, the man was grinning broadly. He seemed to harbor no bad feelings, even though Slocum had whipped (mmm, squeaked by) his pal Gus.

"I hoped to find you here, John," Kraus said. "Wanted a chance to tell ye good-bye."

"You're leaving the camp?" Slocum was genuinely surprised. And disappointed. Abner Kraus was a good man, and Slocum had enjoyed their talks together.

"I am, for a fact, John. For a fact." He was grinning broadly. "Me an' my partners talked it over all evenin' and what we come up with is this. Our claim ain't the very best a man could hope to find. We hear tell there might be better pickings over Idaho way. An' besides, your idea of charging at the gate for that little shindig you an' Gus put together last night, that got us pretty well again an' we might not get so good a chance again if we was to stay here in this camp. So we figure to move on while we can. But I couldn't go without thanking you an' telling you good-bye. That's a fact."

"I'll miss you, Abner. Damned if I won't. You're a good man."

"An' I reckon I would say the same about you, John . . . Wilse." He laughed. "See, I did remember this one last time."

"Watch out for the Indians," Slocum said.

"Oh, we will, never fear. We're going out on the northbound to Bozeman an' then on to Idaho. Got it all figured. An' this way we'll be in enough company on that big Concord to scare off 'most any party of Injun braves. When you decide to pull out, John, you oughta do the same. It only makes sense, you know."

"For a fact," Slocum said, deliberately adopting one of Abner's favorite phrases. He held out his hand. "Luck to you, Abner Kraus."

"An' to you, John Wilse." Abner turned and left, and Slocum watched him go, shaking his head over the eternal optimism of the placer miner.

Strange people, Slocum decided. Always ready to pick up and head for the next strike or the next rumor of a strike. Always hoping to strike it rich with the next turn of a shovel or the next driving of a claim stake.

And hardly ever was there one who actually did make the strike he dreamed of, for placer gold is just not distributed that way, and it is a rare find indeed that makes the effort worth a man's while. But always they believe it, and always they are looking, and a dozen years from now, if the two of them lived so long, Slocum might walk into a placer camp anywhere between here and yonder and find Abner Kraus leaned up against a bar, with the sweat and the muck of the day's diggings still on his clothes and the optimism of the placer miner still in his heart.

Slocum shook his head. Crazy fella. Good fellow. It was a shame he was leaving.

22

Slocum was instantly awake. But he didn't like it. If it was that horny bitch McGee looking for another round of slap-and-tickle he was going to wring her pretty neck. He had spent more than two hours trying to bank her fires just that morning, and now he was a whole hell of a lot more interested in sleep than in a repetition of that action.

"Jus' a minute." He deliberately slurred his words, making himself sound like he was sleep-drugged. It was a precaution born of long habit. If someone outside that door—and why couldn't the silly bastard quit thumping on it?—had something in mind nastier than an afternoon visit, Slocum was willing to take any small advantage he might be able to create. Leading whoever it was into thinking he was sleepwalking when he opened the door just might give Slocum an edge.

With the always ready Colt in his hand, Slocum left the bed and walked with a deliberately heavy tread toward the locked and bolted door, but as he neared it his footsteps softened and he slipped to the side, out of the line of fire. Just in case.

"Wha . . . ?"

The response from the unseen caller—who fi-

nally had quit that infernal racket of knocking and banging on the wood—seemed innocent enough.

"Mr. Wilse? Please, Mr. Wilse, I have a message for you." It was a woman's voice, but not one Slocum recognized.

"Just a minute." Slocum thought, but he was sure he had not heard that particular voice before. He certainly could not place it in Deadwood. It was not Meg McGee, and the only other woman he knew here was Jennifer Porter. As far as he knew she was already gone, had pulled out on the north-bound long hours before. He shrugged and unlocked the door. "Come in."

The Colt was ready, but there was no need for it. It was indeed only a woman who slipped through the open door into his room, closing it behind her.

Slocum gave her a good looking over. He was not particularly impressed by what he saw. The woman was pretty obviously another of Deadwood's professional population. A whore, and judging from her clothing, not a very fancy one at that.

She was not wearing a chemise or kimono like they did up along crib row, but the filthy, ill-fitting dress that drooped from her shoulders was not much above that. She was hard-looking and homely beneath a soiled caking of rice powder, and the rouge-blotched smear of her mouth was surrounded by a ring of pus-weeping open sores.

She had some disease that Slocum would not want to share with her and her customers, he decided, and if she had come here to solicit business she was going to be damned well disappointed.

"What is it?" His tone of voice was not particularly inviting. Nor would the sight of the Colt still in his hand be much of a welcoming gesture. The woman's eyes widened and she stared at the black steel of the gun between them. Neither she nor Slocum was paying much attention to the fact that he was wearing only his drawers.

"Oh," he said. "Nervous? I don't normally shoot people just for waking me up. I won't say it ain't possible, but I'm not likely to do it right now." He turned his back on her—she sure didn't look like she was armed—and returned the Colt to his holster on the bedpost. Slocum sat on the edge of his bed, where he still wished he could be, sound asleep, and waited for her to get around to telling him whatever had brought her here uninvited.

"I, uh, I got a message for you, Mr. Wilse," she repeated. She seemed nervous and was wringing her hands together. That couldn't come from the sight of a nearly naked man, Slocum knew, so she must still be worried about the gun. The hell with her, he thought. He wasn't putting it out of sight for her or anyone else. She could just get over her fears on her own or not at all; that wasn't for him to worry about.

"Go on, woman," he demanded.

She dropped her eyes to the floor and stammered, "Ye . . . yessir. Whatever you say, sir."

Slocum waited. He was annoyed, true, but he had the gift of patience.

"The girl what used to be in the crib nex' to mine, sir," the bawd finally said, "she ast me t' bring you word about somethin', sir."

"The girl in the crib . . . ? Oh, yes. I think I understand. And her name?"

"Jenny, sir. Her name's Jenny. But she ast me t' tell you the message come from a Miss Porter. Does that mean somethin' to you, sir?"

"In a way. So what was the message?"

She looked around, her eyes darting into every

corner of the hotel room before she spoke again. "I don't wanta be involved in this kinda business, if you know what I mean, sir."

Slocum was beginning to wish the idiot bitch had never bothered to waken him. "I *don't* know," he said, "but I'm beginning to get mad. You came this far. Now either tell me what you were told to or get out of here."

"Yessir." She began to redden around the ears. "It's just, if anybody found out . . . an' it was the wrong folks . . ."

"So don't tell them. Now get on with it." Slocum was angry now, and it was probable that she could see that flashing in his eyes. There were few enough armed adult men who could stand up to John Slocum's anger. It was not likely that this low-life crib whore was going to match their nerve.

"Yessir," she said quickly. "An' Jenny, she done me some favors an' . . ."

"I do not care about any of that shit," Slocum said slowly. "Now say your piece and get out of here."

She nodded unhappily. "Miss Jenny, she said fer me t' tell you that there's talk goin' around—I heerd some myself, come to that—that some o' the boys in th' camp here are fixin' to have them a hangin' kind o' party for your dude gamblin' friend, Mr. Lowe. That's the message, sir." She looked acutely uncomfortable and was not looking at him.

"'Who?" It could not be Abner Kraus's friends, Slocum knew. They had pulled out on that north-bound, too. This had to be someone he did not know about.

"Jenny, she didn't say nothin' 'bout that, sir."

"And you? You said you've heard some of the same talk yourself."

The whore bit her lip and looked like she was about to break into tears. She shook her head vigorously and with a sudden squeak of fear turned and fled from the hotel room.

Slocum got up and crossed the now empty room to close and lock the door behind her. He shook his head. Luke Lowe was bad business, and it looked like things were going to get worse for him around Deadwood. Slocum had managed to defuse one threat. He wondered if he would be able to do the same with this other bunch. Whoever they were.

It was time Slocum and Lowe had a downright serious talk, Slocum decided.

And pretty damn soon it was going to be time for Slocum to call his obligations fulfilled and cut loose from that fool cheat of a gambler. The man was more trouble than $50 a week was worth.

23

"Look, Goddammit, I'm telling you, things are getting hot around here for you, Lowe. You've raked an awful lot into your pockets from these fellows, and not all of them are completely stupid. In fact, I'm amazed how long they've let you get away with it."

Lowe looked innocent. Or as close to it as he was able to come. They were seated in the hotel dining room, having a dinner that was their breakfast. When Lowe woke up and was ready for his evening's work he generally came by Slocum's room and the two of them went downstairs to eat.

At least, Slocum thought, the chow had been good on this job. And the McGee. Other than that, though, his responsibilities to Luke Lowe were a bust as far as he was concerned.

"Don't looked so bloody abused, Lowe," Slocum said harshly. "I'm no slouch at the tables myself, and I've seen the way you mechanic those cards. Two minutes into a new deck and you have every fucking one of the face cards marked. Every deck you get away with putting into play is shaved. You can pull an ace any time you need one. You can second-deal with the very best of them. I'll give you that much, Lowe. As a mechanic you are

160

damned good. But you can't get away with a scam that bald for but so long. You got no fucking finesse, Lowe. None. And believe me, I've seen the best. So have some of these boys you've been fleecing. They're onto you, and it's time you thought about getting out of here or I won't be able to protect your cheating ass from them. Hell, man, a squad of infantry with a Gatling gun and Spencer repeaters couldn't protect you once these boys decide to really blow up."

Lowe made a sour face. "Really, Wilse. Or Slocum, if you prefer . . ."

"Don't start in threatening me, Lowe. That right there is about the last thing you want to do now. Like I said, I'm all that's standing between you an' a rope now."

Lowe waved the interruption aside. "I meant no such thing, of course."

Like billy blue hell, Slocum thought.

"It is only that I believe you are overreacting to some crib girl's opium-soaked imagination. If I were cheating—and I categorically deny that I would ever do such a thing—but if I were to, uh, influence the play, I would do it so well that it could not possibly be detected."

The man even managed to look smug when he said it, Slocum saw. Jesus but this was one dumb son of a bitch.

"Fine," Slocum said without really agreeing, "but maybe you ought to think on this then. It don't matter a hill of horseshit if you're the purest of the pure at the tables. If those boys *think* you're a sharp an' a cheat, even if they're wrong, they'll kill you just as dead as if they was right. Mining men are a hard bunch of sons o' bitches," Slocum said. "They don't play once they get good an' pissed off. They just jump up an' *do*. You understand me?"

"Perhaps, perhaps." Lowe still looked unimpressed. But at least Slocum seemed to be beginning to get through to him.

If Slocum only had that stake. . . . But he didn't. And a bag full of "if" won't buy you a cup of coffee.

Lowe started to speak again, but whatever the man might have said was pushed aside by a sudden surge of angry noise from the street outside.

"What the hell is that?" Lowe asked pointlessly.

Slocum was already on his feet, the remains of his meal forgotten on the table before him. "Whatever it is, it sounds damn well serious. I better take a look. Just in case."

Lowe blanched fish-belly white, and a look of stark terror pulled his well-groomed features into an ugly mask. Without a word to Slocum he dashed away from the table and up the stairs toward his room.

No doubt, Slocum thought, locking himself in there with John Slocum expected to stand between his door and the mob if indeed the uproar had anything to do with Luke Lowe.

And it damn sure could, Slocum realized. He sighed. There was only one way to find out. Unconsciously Slocum touched the much used grips of his Colt as he headed for the boardwalk out front to see what the excitement was all about.

It was nothing to do with a minor charlatan like Lowe, Slocum quickly saw.

The crowd of angry—no, furious—men were gathered around a pair of horsemen who sat on fidgeting mounts in the center of the rutted main street of Deadwood. The horsemen looked pale and

strained and just as angry as the men who surrounded them.

Even as Slocum watched, more miners poured
out of the shacks and buildings and alleys along
the street and joined the growing crowd. Most
were shouting questions as they reached the original knot of miners. Slocum joined them.

"Tell it again, Pete," someone called. "These
boys gotta hear about it too."

One of the horsemen stood in his stirrups and
waved for the crowd to be quiet. Amazingly, the
men did settle down to an expectant silence.

"Me and George here just got back from a trip
up to the bank at Bozeman," the man called Pete
said in a loud voice. "We come down the stage
road this afternoon, see. And what we seen up
there is the most God-awful sight I ever hope to
come across."

The crowd was definitely quiet now. Several
more rushed up to join them, but no one was
breaking the silence.

"The northbound coach," Pete said. "It was am-
bushed on the road up there."

A low grumble of restrained hostility began to
rise from the crowd.

"Was it them fuckin' Injuns?" someone in the
crowd yelled.

Pete nodded emphatically. "It damn sure was,
boys. They left some o' their arrers in the coach.
An' what they done to the poor bastards that was
in it, well . . . that ain't Christian to even recall.
It was dirty work, boys. It was them Sioux, all
right. Kilt ever' one of the passengers in that there
coach an' then butchered them like a bunch o'
hawgs. We couldn't even tell for sure who any
o' them might o' been 'cept that there was at
least one woman in the bunch and a mess of

fellas." Pete looked white around the gills at the memory, and for a moment Slocum thought he was going to throw up all over his horse's withers. "Me and George couldn't even be sure how many bodies there was, they was chopped up so bad."

Pete sat down, and the mob around him began to boil again. The men were frightened and they were angry, and they began shouting questions none of which was intelligible from all the rest of the din that rose up around the two horsemen.

"What about the bodies?" someone yelled in a lull in the angrily buzzing sound.

"What about them fucking Injuns?" someone else yelled.

"We need us a posse," another called. "We need to find them heathen savages an' give them back some of their own."

That suggestion raised a howl of approval. The mob had needed nothing else but that purpose, an activity to direct their fears and frustrations and fury.

The mob began to scatter as men ran to find guns and horses and mules that might carry them to the scene of the slaughter.

A chase like that would be a waste of time, Slocum knew. It would be utterly pointless.

The Sioux, rejoicing in their victory, would now be far from the devastated stagecoach, whooping and dancing and bragging to each other about how very brave they had been and about how wonderfully well they had slaughtered the hated whites.

Sons of fucking bitches, Slocum thought.

Normally he had a live-and-let-live attitude when it came to Indians. The way they saw it, they were engaged in warfare, defending what they believed to be theirs. Hell, defending what in a lot of cases really was supposed to be theirs. Including, the way Slocum understood it, these same Black Hills and the sacred Sioux grounds the Black Hills held.

But John Slocum had had friends on that coach. Abner Kraus. His partners. And Miss Jennifer Porter.

The poor girl had been so damned sweet. So hopeful. So intent on making a decent life for herself. She had thought she had a chance and a stake to set it up.

And now she was dead. Her slim, so often abused little body mutilated and destroyed. Her life taken from her. Her hopes and her dreams shattered and drowned in pain and screams and flowing blood.

The thought, of Abner and of Jennifer and of all the others, sent Slocum's blood to the boiling point too, and he was as furious as any of the miners. Perhaps more so. These had been friends of his.

And while he knew full well that there would be no chance to take revenge on a Sioux war party that would no longer be anywhere near, they *had* been friends. And John Slocum could at the very least be there to mourn them and tell them goodbye and see that they were given a decent burial.

Jennifer Porter and Abner Kraus deserved that much, at the very least, even if a burial was all Slocum could do for them now.

Like the others, Slocum turned and began running, looking for a horse or a wagon or whatever it might be that he could beg or borrow or steal if necessary. He was going with that maddened posse, and the hell with Luke Lowe and that prick's problems. Slocum had business of his own to tend to now.

24

"You say they were robbed, too? That doesn't sound like Indians to me."

"I already told you they were," Slocum said. They were in Lowe's suite. Or in what passed for a suite in a raw camp like Deadwood still was. At least it did have two rooms to it. Meg McGee was nowhere in sight. "Every piece of clothing was torn apart at the seams. Every piece of baggage had been hacked open and the contents dumped. Those men were carrying a fair amount of dust with them, I'm sure, but there wasn't any of it to be found when we got there."

Lowe nodded. He did not seem particularly distressed, Slocum noted. Just interested.

As for himself, Slocum did feel distressed. Not by the death he had just seen. There had been too much of that in his past, both during the war and afterward, for mere death to bother him.

Nor even by the unspeakable mutilations the Sioux had inflicted on those corpses. After all, a man can be torn into bloody rags of once-living flesh by a cannonball, and Slocum had seen enough of that long before he ever saw the work of savage Indians. And by now he had seen the worst that the Sioux could do—and the Cheyenne and Kiowa and Comanche and Apache before them.

No, death held no surprises for John Slocum anymore, in any form that inescapable fate might take. What was disturbing him was a sense of . . . loss, of futility. He was genuinely disturbed by the deaths of Abner Kraus and of Jennifer Porter.

And he was disturbed too that he had not even known which of the male bodies he should say his good-byes to. Even having known Abner as well as he had, Slocum had not been able to tell which of the males was Kraus.

The only way he had known which body belonged to Jennifer Porter was because she had been the only woman on the stagecoach. There had been a longer hank of hair still attached to what was left of her scalp and part of a small breast still attached to the mutilated torso that had been hers, a breast that Slocum had so recently caressed and felt pressed warmly against his own chest.

Had it been possible at the moment he saw those things, John Slocum would cheerfully and in good conscience have waved his hands and spoken a set of magical incantations and caused every member of every Sioux nation to fall over dead. Preferably after a week-long agony. Including the smallest of their children.

But Slocum did not bother himself with the impossible, and his patience was as great as his anger. He could wait. Someday he would exact his revenge.

Unlike most of the miners with whom he had been riding, though, John Slocum's deepest hatred was not now with the Sioux who had committed the acts of violence against people who had been John Slocum's friends.

He would harbor scant hatred for a mountain lion that dismembered his best friend, although he would kill the cat if he could. But if some son of a bitch had *induced* that cat to the kill—that man would be John Slocum's avowed enemy to the end of both their days.

And somewhere, Slocum knew, there was a man, a white man, who had induced those Sioux to take the warpath. Some white man who had emboldened them and sent the Sioux into combat by giving them the rifles and the ammunition that had been used in that attack on the stage to Bozeman.

The firepower of the Sioux was amply demonstrated by the shattered wood of the coach, wood entirely too thin to stop the devastating bullets that had left the coach sides a mass of splinters.

Someone had sold those rifles and that ammunition to the Sioux warriors.

Someone had taught them to steal from their victims the coins and the yellow dirt and the bits of paper that had no value at all to a Sioux brave but which would be of such great value to the man who had given them their rifles.

Someone . . .

That man John Slocum wanted to find. *Intended* to find.

Now. Tomorrow. It would not matter. Someday would be soon enough, because Slocum was not likely to forget. Not ever. Not when it came to a debt he chose to assume, and in the matter of Abner Kraus and Jennifer Porter, John Slocum had accepted a blood debt that could be paid in only one coin.

A red film of hatred clouded Slocum's vision, and a cold certainty as unyielding as steel filled his gut, and Lowe had to repeat himself three times before the gambler could bring Slocum's attention back to the hotel room where they sat.

"I'll forgive you for running off like that," Lowe was saying. "But don't let it happen again. I'm paying you to side me. Remember that, mister."

"Go fuck yourself," Slocum said mildly. He really wasn't interested in this boring prick any longer. He had other things to think about.

The gambler looked into Slocum's eyes and swallowed back any retorts he might have made. He cleared his throat, and when he spoke again he spoke in a placating, almost whining tone of voice.

"As it, uh, as it happens, you see, I have decided to accept your advice," Lowe said. "About the mood of the men here in town. Their anger, I mean."

Slocum stared at him, uninterested in what the man might have to say.

"I have decided not to enter the gaming tonight, you see. You said yourself, before the, uh, disturbance last night, that I have milked quite enough out of these men. I have decided you are correct. I will be leaving in the morning. I won't need your services after this evening, Mr. Slocum. I shall, of course, pay you all that is due you."

Slocum gave the gambler a grin that held no humor in it whatsoever. "I never doubted that for a minute, Luke."

Lowe gulped. He seemed to be having difficulty swallowing all of a sudden. "Of course. Of course," he said quickly. "As for this evening, I will be staying in my rooms. But I would like you to, um, keep an eye on things. Until I get clear of the town, that is. I will pay you in the morning. Do you understand?"

"I'm not stupid," Slocum said. "You're scared. You got a right to be scared. Those miners are already upset by all these Indian attacks. They're scared too. Something to take their minds off their other problems, something like hanging a cardsharp, now that would kinda ease their minds some. Yeah, Lowe, I'd say you got a right to be scared. An' you want me to cover your ass until you're safe out of their way. Yeah, I understand that real good, Lowe."

"I'll pay you, of course. I already said that. And a bonus. For tonight. I'll be glad to pay you a bonus for tonight's work. Glad to."

"I'll just bet you will, Luke." Slocum stood and stared coldly down at the gambler. The man seemed smaller now than he had. Fear was causing him to shrink in his chair.

"But I reckon I can use your money," Slocum said. "One more night then." Without a backward glance toward the gambler, Slocum stalked out of the room.

One more night. But now Slocum was not at all certain that he wanted to leave Deadwood. Somewhere around here there was a white man who was selling arms to the Sioux, and Slocum wanted that man.

Somewhere around here or—the idea sounded right when it came to him—maybe somewhere around Bozeman. Somewhere nearer the river transportation that must be used to ship the rifles and the cases of ammunition into this out-of-the-way part of the country. Maybe Bozeman would be a better place to look for the man Slocum wanted to find.

And come morning, Slocum should have the stake he needed to get to Bozeman. That was where he would look first. He could always come back to Deadwood if nothing turned up at that less isolated commercial hub.

Yeah, Slocum thought, that would be the place to look first. And if not there, somewhere else. Anywhere. For as long as the search took.

The end was not subject to the slightest doubt as far as John Slocum was concerned. The end would be death. Only the path was in question now.

25

They came not long after Slocum heard the big
clock in the lobby downstairs strike twelve. He had
no idea how many of them there were, but he
knew what they were up to long before he ever got
a look at any of them. Anyone with a right to be
in that upstairs hallway would have come in and
walked up the stairs with little if any concern
about the sounds his footsteps might make. These
men came creeping up the stairs, their presence
announced by the shifting creak of the poorly
nailed treads.

Slocum stood up from the chair he had dragged
into the hall and cat-footed across the bare wood
of the floor to conceal himself against the wall
where they were not likely to see him when they
reached the upstairs landing.

There was little light in the hall. Only one lamp
was burning to mark the landing. But there was
enough for Slocum's purposes.

The men reached the top of the stairs and
moved directly across the landing toward Luke
Lowe's closed and barred door. There were five of
them, and they seemed to know exactly where
they were headed. Slocum wondered if the clerk
downstairs might have tipped them about where

to find Lowe's room. He must have, Slocum decided.

In their confidence—overconfidence—the five men did not even look around, never once glanced around to see Slocum or the empty chair placed outside Slocum's door. They crept across the hall floor and gathered outside the door to the best suite in the hotel. One of them took something out of his pocket. A key, Slocum saw with no particular surprise. So they had indeed bribed the desk clerk. Probably there would be more of them waiting downstairs with a rope. Outside the hotel lobby, of course. The management would not want it known that they participated in the murder of one of their paying guests. That would be bad for future business, after all.

Slocum grinned. The stupid bastards were apt to earn him a bigger bonus than Luke Lowe intended to pay.

"Think about it first, boys," Slocum said in a low voice. He sounded quite cheerful, actually. After the past couple of days, a little violence and bloodletting would do his heart good. Let him get rid of some of the frustrations he'd been feeling.

And unlike Abner Kraus and his partners, these fellows were no particular friends of John Slocum. They might have been better off if they had been.

The softly spoken words seemed to have a chilling effect on the five would-be vigilantes. They froze in place with their hands halted entirely too far—for their comfort, not Slocum's—from the butts of the revolvers dangling in crude pouches at their belts.

"Any or all of you is welcome to try it," Slocum invited. His voice remained just as soft and calm as it had been.

The men turned to face him, but all they could

see was an indistinct form in the shadows of the hall. They were much nearer the single lamp than he was, and they undoubtedly knew it.

"We got no quarrel with you, mister," one of the men said.

"Think again," Slocum told him.

Another, apparently of a more incautious nature, began to get angry. "We told you, mister, our quarrel's not with you. It's with that bastard inside. He's been cheating us at the card tables. We figure to have our money back."

Another, emboldened, spoke up then. "And then some," he snapped. "With a rope. A man your age oughta know better than to get between a necktie party an' its guest of honor. Unless you want an invitation too."

Several of the men were sneering now. They were beginning to feel better about the situation. After all, there were five of them. And only one of Slocum. They had him outgunned good and proper. Any sensible man would back away from those odds.

On the other hand, Slocum was not always known for being sensible in the face of odds that would have sent any other man scurrying for cover.

"There's five of you," Slocum stated the obvious. "And I got six shells in this Colt. Now make up your minds, boys. You're disturbing my sleep."

One of the men laughed, and the others seemed to take heart from that. After all, no one could take down five men with six shots. Nobody was that good. Certainly no no-name called Wilse who hadn't been heard of before and who wasn't likely to be heard of again after this night. They all understood that, didn't they?

"Go on, fella," one of the vigilantes said. "Back

out of here now, and we'll leave you alone. You can get out of Deadwood in the morning."

Slocum stayed where he was. To all intents and purposes he seemed to be lounging against the wall. Certainly he did not seem upset or frightened. Nor did he seem to be going anywhere. He just stood there. Waiting.

"We're going in there now," one of them said. "We're going to fetch that cheat out and have a talk with him."

Slocum shrugged. He had given them all the warning he intended to. Whatever they did now was up to them.

The man with the key turned back to the door and reached to insert it in the lock while his partners kept an eye on Luke Lowe's bodyguard.

A gunshot exploded in the stillness of the narrow hall. The sound echoed and reverberated through the small space, bouncing off the walls and filling the confined area with magnified power.

The man with the key was no longer standing outside Lowe's door. He dropped like a fallen sack of flour and spilled into an awkward heap at the foot of the door, blocking it. There was a mushy gray-and-red pudding where his head had been.

None of the remaining four had seen Slocum's gun hand move, but now he stood facing them with the Colt in his grip. And the gaping barrel leveled at them.

Three of them stood rooted and pale, but the shock and the fear galvanized one of the four into foolish action. He tried for the revolver that hung at his belt, and again the heavy Colt roared.

The loud thump of a falling carcass announced that now there were three.

Those three should have—and could have—

walked away from it then, but the sound of the second shot was too much for them.

In a panic the three vigilantes tried to out-muscle this tall, lean, hawk-faced man who was so fast and so sure. As one, their hands swept toward their guns.

This time the response was like a roar of thunder rolling through the narrow hallway, and the three were turned from men into so many hunks of cooling meat that littered the hall floor.

Without a change in his expression, Slocum turned from Lowe's door and stepped to the head of the stairs.

The desk clerk was racing up those stairs, grabbing the handrail and catapulting himself forward. There was anxiety etched on his thin features but no fear. Not yet.

Something had gone wrong, and he did not know what, but he was much more angry than afraid. Those bastards had *promised* him they would take the gambler outside to do their work. They had promised there would be no disturbance that might upset the rest of the hotel guests. And now all this shooting and such. The whole damn hotel was going to be awake and upset, and all their complaints would fall on the clerk's head. Damn it, those boys had *promised*.

The scrawny fellow ran up the flight of stairs and straight into John Slocum's gun barrel.

The muzzle of the Colt, still hot from its spew-ing death, was shoved hard against the bridge of tender flesh between the desk clerk's nose and upper lip. The man's eyes widened as fear re-placed anger, and he halted in mid-leap with two steps to go to the top.

"Je . . . Je . . . Jesus," he spit out. "Wha . . . ?"

"You oughta know," Slocum said mildly. "You gave 'em the key."

The thoroughly frightened clerk tried to shake his head in a futile denial, but the pressure of that hot, smoky Colt barrel held his head rigidly still.

"Did you count the shots, neighbor?" Slocum asked casually. "If you did, you'll know if I spent five shells or six putting those boys down."

Slocum grinned down into the clerk's eyes, and the sight of it was enough to send a dark, wet stain spreading down the man's right pantleg.

"Those *were* a bunch of robbers that jumped me, wasn't they? Sure they was. Had to be. In a respectable *ho*-tel like this one. Wasn't they?"

"Yu . . . yu . . . yes," the clerk croaked.

"I thought so," Slocum said. "Now do me a favor before you send somebody up to clean up the mess on your pretty floor here."

"Y-y-yessir?"

"Go outside. Do it yourself, mind, so I know it's done right. Go outside and tell these boys' friends they'd best go get themselves some sleep. Tomorrow's likely to be a long day, and I know they've got lots of work to do then. They really need their rest tonight. An' they don't have to worry about are things okay in the hotel tonight. You can tell 'em I'll be right here keepin' an eye on things all night long. You will do that for me, won't you?"

"Yessir. Of course, sir. I . . . anything you want." A grimace of terror that probably was intended to be a placating smile pulled the clerk's lips back away from his teeth. "I wouldn't want any of our guests to be concerned, sir."

"I didn't think you would," Slocum said. "Now go tell those boys. Tell them they won't be needing their rope. And then get somebody to help you haul these bodies out of here. I know it's pretty dry up in this country, but bodies do start to stink after a while, you know."

"Yessir." The clerk swallowed hard and began to back cautiously down the stairs, one step at a time. His wide-open eyes never once left Slocum or that gaping, lethal gun barrel.

26

Lowe was a badly shaken man. Dark circles bagged under his eyes, and there were deep lines of strain pulling at the corners of his mouth and eyes as well. He looked like he had not slept for a moment the night before. Certainly he had not had a moment's peace since midnight.

Meg McGee was finishing their packing, cramming the things they had bought since their arrival in Deadwood into a pair of newly acquired carpetbags that showed a great deal of previous use. This was the first time in more than a week that Slocum could remember seeing the woman fully dressed, but now she was wearing the same traveling gown that he had first seen her in, although considerably cleaner now, and after major repairs had been made. There were few items of women's apparel available in the camp of Deadwood. A lady just had to make do.

"I . . . I need your help, Slocum," Lowe was insisting.

"Don't call me that."

"Yes, sorry. Of course. Mr. Wilse. But I do truly need your help. Just until I get to Bozeman, you understand. Just a few more days."

"Pay me what you owe me, Lowe. Including that

bonus." Slocum grinned. It was not a pretty sight. "I expect you're going to be generous, Lowe."

"Of course. I intended to be. You *know* that." The gambler fumbled inside his suit coat and pulled out a fat wallet stuffed with currency. He stripped out a wad of bills and shoved them toward Slocum without counting them.

Slocum was not shy about counting what was his. He took his time examining the sheaf of fives and tens and an occasional twenty. The amount came to something over $200. It was damn sure enough for a stake out of Deadwood.

"I met my obligations to you, Luke. We're quits now," Slocum said.

"No." The man sounded like he was on the thin edge of panic. "Please. I'll pay you. I'll pay you well. Just until we get clear of Deadwood. Not even all the way to Bozeman. Just one day's ride, Sl . . . Mr. Wilse. That's all I ask. One day's ride north."

"There's Indians up that way."

Lowe shook his head violently from side to side. "I know a shortcut. Off the stage road. An old trail between here and Bozeman. Nobody uses it anymore. The Sioux won't be watching the trail. If they're still around they'll be watching the stage road, looking for another stage or party of whites to jump."

"They'll know about the trail. Hell, they prob'ly made it. You can't tell me they won't know about it," Slocum said.

Lowe agreed quickly. Slocum thought the prick probably would have agreed to anything Slocum said right then. "Of course they know. But they'll be watching the stage road. It will be perfectly safe. I wouldn't go myself if that weren't true."

Slocum grinned at him. "Luke, you ain't gonna

be safe here nor there either one. Now that's a fact, old son."

"I'll pay you. I'll pay you well. I'll pay you in advance. Right now, if you like. Just help me get away from these miners. That's all I ask. Not even all the way to Bozeman. Just one day's ride. I'll pay you two hundred dollars, Mr. Wilse. Two hundred. In gold coin, if you like. Hard money." He reached into another pocket and dragged out a handful of shining double eagles.

Slocum looked at the coins and smiled. By God there was something particularly satisfying about the sight of a double eagle. Something beyond the gold it was made of or the $20 value of the coin. There was something about the double eagle that was just plain pretty. The things were hard to resist. Which Lowe undoubtedly knew as well as Slocum did.

Actually, Slocum had decided the night before that he was going to go to Bozeman anyway. Getting paid to escort Luke Lowe there was just a bonus on top of his bonus.

But Lowe needn't know that. Now that all the obligations were quits it was no skin off Slocum's balls if he stung the gambler some.

"You're way short," Slocum said. "Two hundred ain't half enough."

"Five hundred, then. Five hundred. Right now. I don't have that much coin. I'll give you all I have in coin. The rest in currency. Or in dust. Whatever you prefer. Five hundred, Sl . . . Wilse. Right now."

Slocum shrugged. "All right, five hundred."

"Yes. Right now." Lowe handed Slocum the entire handful of double eagles. They added up to $360. For the rest the gambler dug into a well-stuffed money belt full of currency and small pouches of gold dust.

Judging from the bulk of that money belt and the thickness of the wallet in Lowe's coat, the man must be carrying one hell of a lot of money on him. One bitch of an amount.

Slocum wondered just how far his obligations were going to stretch for this petty, mean, miserable gambler. It wouldn't be right to pop the son of a bitch between the eyes and take his money as long as Slocum was in his employ. But that would end after one day's ride from Deadwood, wouldn't it? Sure it would. The man had said so himself. Just one day's ride and they were quits.

And if their trails happened to cross again, say between the first night's camp and Bozeman, there wouldn't be any big reason why Slocum shouldn't do Lowe the favor of removing some of the burden from the man. Making sure the poor fellow didn't have so much weight to carry.

"One day's ride, right, Lowe?"

"One day. That's all. After that you can ride on about your own business. Just get me clear of Deadwood and these damned miners."

"It's a deal, Mr. Lowe," Slocum said. He looked over Lowe's shoulder and winked at the delectable Meg McGee.

Maybe, he was thinking, when—if, that is—he happened to run into Lowe again afterward, maybe McGee would like to ride along with him for a while. There were some sights down in Denver that he wouldn't mind showing her. Like the ceiling of a hotel or two he knew down there. *Real* hotels, not like this rat-trap excuse for one that Deadwood offered. Places with beds so soft ol' Meg wouldn't have to get out of them for a week at a time.

"One day's ride," he said.

"Thank you. Thank you, John. I'll always appreciate what you are doing for me, what you've already done for me."

Slocum grinned. That business outside Luke's door seemed to have put the squirrelly bastard into a very reasonable humor this morning.

"And you will, of course, provide me with a horse," Slocum prodded for that one final inch. "I can't hardly go along and help you if I'm not mounted proper, can I?"

As expected, Lowe agreed immediately. "The finest horse in Deadwood. I guarantee it." He shoved his shirttails back in place over the thick money belt and patted his clothes into some semblance of order. "Can we go now? Right away?"

"Whatever you say, Lowe." Slocum grinned that evil grin of his. "After all, you're the boss."

27

The trail was damned sure well off the semifrequently traveled stage road. As a matter of fact, Slocum was more than wondering just how in the hell a tinhorn gambler like Luke Lowe would ever have known of it.

Most of it was barely discernible in the thinning grass of the prairie after they left the heavily wooded, heavily watered protrusions of the Black Hills behind them and crossed the skimpy flow of water that was the Belle Fourche River at this time of year.

They were making good time, and Lowe sure seemed to know what he was doing and where he was going, Slocum saw. The man had guided them better than an army scout could have done, and he never once seemed to hesitate on which way to turn next or how to find the easiest crossing over one dusty dry wash after another.

All of a sudden Slocum was having difficulty trying to understand this miserable cheat who'd been paying him. Back in Deadwood—and before then for that matter—Lowe had seemed just another cheap gambler on the cheat, dragging down dishonestly earned money by the double handful and in his element across a gaming table. Now the bastard wasn't acting like that at all. Slocum just plain couldn't figure him.

Meg McGee, now that was a different story. The woman was riding decorously sidesaddle, as would be expected from her ladylike dress, but there the appearances of gentility stopped completely. She was nervous and whining and complaining like a spinster lady whose Great Dane has been castrated by a bunch of mean-minded little boys. Seemed like all the joy had gone out of Meg McGee's life all of a sudden, and Slocum couldn't figure that either.

He would have thought that the prospect of reaching a reasonably civilized place like Bozeman, where she could get some properly fancy clothes to replace the ones that had been lost during the stagecoach fight a while back, well, Slocum would have expected that to make up for just about any amount of suffering she had to go through on the way there. After all, he had come to know her pretty well in the past week and a half, and he thought he could figure her out about as well as any man can ever figure a woman—which may not be so damned well at the best of times, but which still surprised him when he found himself this far off the mark.

Instead of being eager about the prospect of reaching Bozeman, Meg seemed awfully nervous, and her nervousness seemed to be showing itself in all the bitching she was doing. After all, Slocum figured, *no*body could be *that* uncomfortable after so short a period of time in the well-padded sidesaddle Lowe had been able to scrounge for her back in Deadwood.

Regardless, Slocum thought, the threat of interference from the angry miners should be well behind them now, and in a few more hours John

Slocum would be completely quit of Luke Lowe
and his pretty house pet.

He smiled to himself. Out of his obligations to
the man, if not completely quit of him, anyway.
After that, whatever Slocum might choose to do—
and how he might choose to bankroll himself—
would be his own affair. He would owe Lowe not
one damned thing after they made camp.

The traveling party of three reached the edge
of a rocky, tree-studded hill that must have been
an outrider for the crowd when the Black Hills
were formed. Again Lowe seemed to know exactly
where he was going and what he was doing. He
led them around the east side of the hill, away
from what Slocum would have thought would be
the most direct and logical route toward Bozeman,
to the banks of a lively flowing little stream that
came seeping out of the side of the hill a few hundred yards upslope from where Lowe drew rein.

"This will do for tonight," Lowe announced.

Slocum looked at him sharply, again surprised
by the man's decision. "There's still more than an
hour of daylight left," Slocum observed aloud.

"There is," Lowe agreed. "But this is the best
water for at least five hours' travel. We'll stop
here." There was no uncertainty in the man's
voice at all. His decision was made, and this was
where they would stay. Lowe stepped down from
his horse and began pulling the saddle.

"I reckon this is as far as you've hired me,
then," Slocum said. He got off the stout-bodied
grulla Lowe had found for him—the horse was
decent, but the saddle was downright sorry—and
began helping the woman down from her leggy
yellow horse.

Lowe was already busy setting up a camp of
sorts, pulling utensils and food out of his bulging

saddlebags and making a fuss about the camp arrangements. One of the carpetbags was tied on behind his cantle and the other rode behind Meg's. The man had not bought a pack animal and probably had not been able to find one that suited him, or perhaps one that its owner had been willing to part with. He certainly had enough money on him that he could have made the travel arrangements more comfortable than he had.

"I reckon I'll ride on for those few hours," Slocum said as soon as the gear behind Meg McGee's saddle had been unstrapped and placed near the spot where Lowe was building the wood needed for a fire. "And if I was you," he added, "I wouldn't be so quick to show smoke around here. I know you got faith in them Sioux being elsewhere, but only a fool would count on it."

Lowe looked alarmed, but the expression had come onto his face before Slocum ever mentioned the Indians.

"You can't leave," the gambler said.

"Maybe you don't remember as good as I do, then, but we agreed on one day's ride. You just done that, mister. I figure from here on my time's my own."

"No I . . . I didn't mean anything like that. Not at all." Lowe was keeping a wary eye on Slocum's gun hand. John Slocum's reputation probably would have been enough. After that little demonstration of the night before, facing and taking five armed men in the hall outside Lowe's door, there was very little likelihood that Luke Lowe was going to do anything to make Slocum seriously annoyed.

"I'm sure you didn't," Slocum purred.

"No, I . . . just meant that, well, we have good food here and good water. You have to sleep somewhere. I just thought tomorrow morning might be more convenient all the way around." He smiled. It looked very much a forced smile, but he managed it. "I am trying to be hospitable, Mr. Wilse. And I assure you, I was correct about the water."

It was true, Slocum conceded, that there was no canteen hanging from his saddle rigging. And it was equally true that he did not want to lose contact with Luke Lowe's small traveling party. For reasons of his own.

Meg McGee clinched it for him. The woman came rushing to his side with a pleading look in her huge violet eyes. "Please, John. I would feel *ever* so much more comfortable if you were to stay with us. Just for tonight."

She had placed herself between Slocum's body and Lowe's, and with her own trim frame concealing her from Lowe's view she allowed the carefully tended nails of one hand to trail playfully over Slocum's crotch. The invitation was undeniable.

And, Slocum admitted to himself, interesting. She was, after all, one very fine fuck.

She was also Luke Lowe's woman, bought and paid for, if not necessarily faithful, and how she proposed to slip away from the gambler across a few firelit paces of campsite and tuck into the kip with Slocum was an interesting question indeed.

Better not count too heavily on that, Slocum thought. After tomorrow, when Slocum had all the money in his jeans, would be a better time for him to think about in terms of enjoying Meg McGee's lovely body.

"Please," she whispered, still toying with the buttons on his fly.

How Lowe could have missed the implications of what his woman was up to was beyond Slocum

—and why the female should have gotten so bold all of a sudden—but miss them he evidently did. Slocum looked past the woman to the gambler, and there was certainly no trace of displeasure on the man's face.

Slocum had no doubt at all that Lowe would be afraid to brace him. The man was hardly a model of bravery. But Slocum seriously doubted that Lowe would be a good enough actor to so completely withhold his feelings if he knew what his woman was doing and took exception to it.

This whole damn business with Lowe and Meg, ever since they left Deadwood, was entirely unlike what Slocum would have expected based on everything else he had come to know about the two. But come morning, he thought, there would be no reason why he should care in the slightest.

And, really, there was no reason now why he could not share their camp for this one night. Then in the morning he could drag iron, accept his "winnings," and be on his way, with or without the fair lady and her horny habits.

He shrugged. "All right. I'll stay the night. But come morning we go our own ways."

"Of course, of course." Lowe was smiling. For some reason he even looked . . . relieved, Slocum thought. Definitely odd. "No obligations," Lowe said.

"You got it. No obligations. You said it yourself." Slocum restrained himself from adding, "remember that."

28

"I'm feeling a little nervous and out of sorts. I think I'll take a hike up that hill there, maybe find a rock to sit on and do some thinking. If I'm not back by the time you go to sleep, don't wait up for me." Lowe was speaking to Meg, but his words were pitched loud enough—deliberately? Slocum had the impression that might be so, but he could not understand why—for Slocum to hear also.

Damn. All of a sudden Luke Lowe was acting like anything *but* what Slocum expected.

Yet this wasn't any kind of setup. Slocum was dead certain of that. The man turned and walked out of the camp into the newly fallen darkness without adding even a belly gun to his usual concealed gambler's belly-range armament. If he had taken a rifle along, Slocum might have thought the fool intended to circle back and have a go at the famous outlaw. Slocum sure would not put it past the man to want to collect a reward on a scalp labeled J. Slocum. But that just couldn't be, with Lowe walking away the next thing to unarmed.

Come to think of it, Slocum decided, that in itself was damned odd. Given any choice at all, Slocum knew that *he* would never be dumb enough to walk out from here unarmed. Not even in search of a bush to crap behind.

Lowe definitely was acting strangely this evening. All day long, really.

Slocum had little time to ponder the gambler's oddities, though. Lowe was barely out of sight in the gloom before Meg McGee was on her feet and approaching Slocum.

"Thank goodness, John dear. I was afraid we might have trouble finding some time to ourselves. With Luke out walking, well . . ." She had an enticing smile spread over her pretty face, and she was already unbuttoning the bodice of her gown.

"What if . . . ?"

"Oh, don't be a spoilsport now, John. Shush." Meg had switched on every ounce of her not inconsiderable sensuality. She was practically oozing raw sex, and she slipped the fabric from her shoulders, exposing an extraordinary pair of high, firm, globular breasts. "I know Luke. Much better than you do, dear. When he is in a mood like this, and thank goodness they are rare, the poor dear might be gone for hours. He might not return before dawn." She shrugged. "I'll not complain. Not this time. This time, you see, it gives me a last opportunity to be with you and that marvelous tool you have swinging between your legs, love."

An invitation like that, coming from a woman as beautiful as Meg McGee . . . John Slocum was not going to turn it down. No way. He stood and began to unbutton his shirt.

"Here. Let me help you." Meg tossed her gown aside and for a brief moment posed in front of him, obviously quite fully aware of her own beauty and desirability.

She dropped to her knees in the dust of the campsite and began with practiced fingers to flip open the buttons of his fly. In seconds the full length of him sprang free and upright, throbbing lightly in his anticipation of her.

Meg leaned forward and began to lick him with slow, lingering strokes that he found irresistible and maddeningly exciting.

She looked up at him and smiled. "I want to take my time with you tonight, dear. I want to explore and enjoy every square inch of your skin. I want to feel you inside me every way it is possible for a man to enter a woman. *Every* way. Do you understand what I'm telling you, dear? I want you every way possible. Everywhere." She laughed. "All at the same time, if you can think of a way to manage it."

Slocum's mind was hardly on rational analysis at the moment. And with good reason. With half of the immense length of his erect cock buried in Meg's warm, willing mouth, he could be readily forgiven for thinking primarily about what the lovely gambler's mistress was doing to him.

Yet in some dim, scarcely active corner of his brain, Slocum found this too to be odd. As odd, perhaps, as Luke Lowe's behavior since they left Deadwood.

During the past week and a half Slocum had balled Meg McGee daily and had enjoyed every moment of it. But it would not have been possible for him to have done that without becoming at least somewhat aware of the woman's tastes and preferences when it came to bedroom performances.

She liked, for instance, oral sex. She positively adored having him ram himself vigorously into her from on top while she twined her legs around him and raked his back with ecstatic fingernails. She leaped and bucked and thrashed with every bit as much vigor as he did while he fucked her.

But during that time she had never once shown any inclination to have him enter her Greek style up the small brown chute. Not once.

Now she seemed to be demanding that of him, too.

Strange, Slocum thought, while he was still capable of thought.

A moment later he was not. She had drawn him down onto the ground, on top of her magnificently voluptuous body. Guiding him, rising to meet him, urging him deeper and ever deeper into her hot, dripping sex.

Slocum plunged himself into her, and it was like being swallowed whole by an enormous pussy. Every part of her, from scalp to toenails, was on this woman a sexual organ, and she used all of herself to draw him ever deeper and ever hotter until he could see and feel and think nothing but Meg McGee.

He grabbed her melonlike breasts, one in each strong hand, and raised himself up on stiffened arms so he could watch the pleasure wash over her beautiful face while he squeezed and twisted and slammed his meat into her.

The whole woman was one large fucking machine, and Slocum matched her stroke for wild stroke until an explosion began to build deep inside his balls and burst outward, spewing his steaming jism deep inside her, with all the force of a holiday rocket bursting into red and green fireworks on the Fourth of July.

Meg screamed out hs name in her own fierce, mad climax, and she raked his back over and over in her passion.

As he collapsed, spent, on top of that gorgeous

body, Slocum hoped Luke Lowe had had time to get out of hearing distance, because there wasn't a man alive who could have mistaken that cry for anything but what it was.

And he hoped he could find a soft patch of earth this night that did not require that he sleep on his damned back. It might be quite a while before he was healed enough for comfort there.

He sighed and lifted his sweat-dripping chest away from the pillow formed by her breasts. He shook his head and looked into her large violet eyes.

"Lady," he said, "you are some kinda good fuck, you know that?"

"Thank you, kind sir, the lady says," Meg told him. She laughed and stretched.

He was still inside her, although softer now, and the movement caused him to begin to slip out of the warm, dripping socket of her body.

"Ohhhh," she pouted, "don't take it away. I still have plans for that pretty thing, you know."

"Do ye now?" he asked. "And to think, you're the one should know how dead it is 'cause you're the one has killed it."

"Killed? I don't think so. Sleeping? Perhaps. But I do believe I can resurrect the darling monster." She laughed again. "Here, let me show you how."

She wriggled out from under him and pressed him down on the ground. He flinched at the pain but quickly forgot it. With tantalizing expertise she bent to him and began quickly to prove that he was still fully capable so soon after that tremendous explosion he had just experienced.

"Damned if you aren't right at that," he admitted. "Though I never would have believed it if I hadn't seen it for myself."

"May I take that as a compliment, then?"

"You may, and then some. Usually it takes me a *little* while anyhow."

"Oh, but I hardly believe that, John Slocum. You're a stallion. A bull. I refuse to imagine this marvelous thing any way but the way it is right now . . . tall and firm and as ready as a buck rabbit."

"Shut up and prove your point," he told her with a laugh.

And she did. Expertly. She swirled him inside her rouged lips and nibbled him and drew him deeper and deeper, bobbing her head in time to wave after crashing wave of sensation until he thought he would explode.

And explode he did. As powerfully as before or even more so, and the woman sat up smiling broadly and made a show of wiping the juices from her chin with perfectly manicured fingers which she then slowly, languorously licked while she stared into Slocum's appreciative eyes.

"There," she said with evident satisfaction. "I told you so."

"Haven't you ever heard it ain't polite to say 'I told you so'?"

"I've heard that, yes. But I'm not done proving my point." She chuckled. "We still have one more way to go, dear heart. One more time."

"Now I really *don't* believe it," Slocum said.

"Oh, you can believe it all right. And I do intend to prove it to you." She rose lightly to her feet and stood over him with her body provocatively on display for him to admire.

In spite of himself, Slocum felt a faint stirring of renewed vigor just from looking at her. Oh, she was fine, he was thinking. Prime.

"Wait right there, dear. I want to find some lotion or something to ease the way." She laughed.

"Grease from a rind of bacon if nothing else. I'll be right back."

She left him and began rummaging through the duffel they had unloaded from the horses. While she was doing that, Slocum had a moment to think without her expert, demanding sexuality to cloud his thoughts, and the more he thought, the odder this night seemed.

Meg. Lowe. Neither of them was acting at all the way they should.

There was something off-key here. Something wrong. The thought struck him abruptly, and he did not like it when it did. Something . . . sinister? Was there a reason why Lowe walked out so conveniently? And why Meg McGee was so intent on keeping him occupied in ways that had never interested her before?

It was possible, Slocum conceded. The man who is utterly irresistible to a beautiful woman may only have a bigger bankroll than the other fellow. And since that was not the truth in this particular case, there could well be some other compelling reason.

Like, for instance, Luke Lowe ordering his woman to keep the gunman occupied while Lowe . . . While Lowe *what*?

What could the sneaking bastard be up to on a hillside way the hell out in the middle of nowhere with nothing but coyotes and jackrabbits and . . . Jesus! And maybe some Sioux Indians around for company.

Slocum jumped to his feet and began dragging on his discarded clothes.

Meg McGee could wait a little while longer if she wanted one more fuck from J. Slocum. The gentleman in question was about to take himself a hike up a hill.

29

"You can't leave."

"What?" Slocum could hardly believe what he had just heard. "What did you say?"

"I said, you cannot leave camp. Not now. I'm sorry."

"Lowe's orders?"

She shrugged. Impulsively—except that he doubted that now, too—she ran to him and began to cover his mouth with hot, demanding kisses. "It doesn't matter, John. Nothing matters. Except what we have here. You said yourself I'm good. Let me show you just *how* good I can be, dear." She gave him a seductively lewd wink. "I'll prove it. Again."

All of a sudden she looked only lewd to him. There was no longer any seductiveness left in the woman's transparently phony come-ons.

"Let go of me, Meg. I want to take a walk."

She began to look desperate. "Please, John. You don't know the trouble I'll get into if . . ."

"At least you do admit Lowe ordered me kept here. Is that supposed to be in your favor, Meg? It isn't working, you know. And I'm still leaving."

"Please!" She sounded genuinely afraid now.

Incredibly, Meg McGee leapt away from him then. She darted toward Slocum's saddle, where his

Winchester lay in its scabbard. She bent and began trying to pull the heavy weapon free of the leather.

"Shee-it," Slocum said.

Calmly he strode to her and pulled her up by the shoulders. She began to fight with him then, scratching at his eyes and slapping at his face until he realized there was no logical way he was going to be able to calm her down.

Whatever was going on here, whatever orders Luke Lowe had given her and for whatever reasons, something was badly wrong, and he wanted to find out what it was.

Meg absolutely would not calm down or leave him alone, and Slocum was no longer in any mood to baby or protect her. He raised his arm and clubbed her with his open hand.

She spun away and dropped to her knees, stunned but not unconscious.

Bitch, he thought.

He did not dare leave her here alone in the camp. He could take his Winchester with him, but he had no idea how many guns Lowe might have stashed in his bag and hers. And Slocum was not sure he had time enough to conduct a search. Besides, he was angry, plain and simple.

With no regard now for whether he might hurt her delicate flesh, Slocum dragged her bodily to the side of the camp and found some lengths of packing strings in the kitchen gear Lowe had dumped onto the ground earlier.

Without another word to her he tied Meg McGee hand and foot and started to walk away.

"Please!"

There was no point in arguing with her about a need for silence. That would be wasted time, Slocum decided. He wheeled, found a rag, and stuffed it into her mouth. He secured it in place with another rag tied around her pretty head. If she strangled, the hell with her. It would be her own damned fault.

"Now," he muttered with satisfaction.

Slocum began picking his way swiftly and silently up the hillside in the direction Luke Lowe had taken when he left the camp some time earlier.

Slocum had no idea how long the man had been gone, but it must have been an hour or perhaps longer. That would give him a long lead if he had kept on the move all that time.

On the other hand, Slocum doubted that Lowe would have planned an extensive walk. Wherever he was going and whatever the man was up to, there had to be some entirely logical reason for it. And Slocum was betting that that reason would not be too far away from the campsite Lowe so obviously had had in mind even before they left Deadwood. They had not come to this camp by any accident, and it seemed clear enough that Lowe must have been here before in the past. Certainly he had had no trouble finding his way despite his city-slicker gambler's image.

Slocum just wished to hell he had some faint, vague idea of what was going on.

By the time Slocum was a hundred yards from camp he had completely forgotten about the bound and gagged woman he had left behind. His concentration now was entirely on what lay ahead of him in the direction Lowe had taken.

Wooded hillsides are foreign to most cowhands and other men of the open western plains, but to John Slocum they were a step back in time, back to the squirrel woods where he had spent so many hours as a boy in search of sport and, not so incidentally, in search of meat for the family table.

He had been good in the woods then, able to

stalk his prey in almost total silence, even in the fall when the crisp newly dropped leaves under-foot made silent movement the most difficult.

Here, where all the major growth was ever-green, with its deep underlying carpet of decaying needles to cushion sound, Slocum was able to move like a ghost from tree to concealing tree.

He still had no idea which direction he should take, but he climbed quickly, allowing his senses to reach out into the dark silence that surrounded him.

There was no trail to follow here, would have been none in that thick pad of fallen needles even if it had been broad daylight, but the senses other than eyesight are at their most acute in the dark-ness, and Slocum had long since learned to trust his instincts. If there was no visible trail there might be something else. A sound carrying far on the crisp night air. A quick crash of game spooked by something unseen ahead of him. A scent rising from the . . .

Slocum stopped dead in his tracks, his body as alertly poised as that of a good bird-hunting pointer. He lifted his head toward the sky and flared his nos-trils, drawing the cool air deep into his lungs. He exhaled with slow deliberation and did it again.

Smoke. He wasn't sure. He wasn't at all sure. But there seemed to be a faint hint of woodsmoke on the softly moving night air.

The breeze was so slight that he was not posi-tive even which direction it was coming from. He used the ancient and honorable expedient of wet-ting his finger and holding it out before him.

That way. He thought. He slid forward once again, this time angling his course to the left and no longer climbing the hillside that continued to jut above him.

He moved more slowly now, much more cautiously. If he was right . . .

He got another, stronger whiff of the scent. He was sure now that it was smoke. And there sure as hell didn't seem to be any glow in the sky that would warn of a far-off prairie fire.

Moving with the infinite caution now of a man who expects any shadow to shoot at him, Slocum cat-footed his way forward once again. Each step now seemed to make the smoke scent clearer to him, although he could not yet see any bright gleam of flames that might pinpoint its origin.

As silent as morning mist drifting over the surface of a sleepy river, Slocum glided forward in the darkness. He moved onward like that for what seemed an incredible distance before he finally caught sight of a distant flicker of dancing flame and could know where the airborne trail was leading him.

He came near the fire and bellied down onto the soft carpet of the pine-studded hillside to slither forward cautiously, ever more slowly, knowing that this was precisely the kind of curiosity that could kill the cat. Yet never once thinking about turning back before he found out what Luke Lowe might be up to out here in the middle of nothing, where even an expert cartographer might be unsure if he was in Dakota or Wyoming or even Montana Territory.

The surprise, when finally he did see who was gathered around the fire that lay ahead of him, was enough to make John Slocum suck in his breath in spite of the iron-willed control he was keeping over himself.

Luke Lowe was there all right.

And he was anything but alone.

30

There were twenty of them, perhaps more. Slocum did not take the time to count them. They
were quite a genial crowd too, laughing and smoking and having a fine old time. Luke Lowe was
right there in the middle of them. The guest of
bloody honor at the evening's gathering. Laughing
along with them. Smoking with them. Apparently
having just as fine a time as they were.

Sioux Indians. Sioux *warriors,* by God. Young
men in their late teens and early twenties. Happy
men. Excited.

They were, by God, on a shopping spree. And
they were enjoying it as much as any New York
debutante given free rein with her father's credit.

Slocum was *sure* that was what they were doing.
And that fucking Luke Lowe was right in there
ready to reap some profits from them.

On a blanket spread out before the fire Slocum
could see a hefty collection of gold-dust pokes,
loose piles of currency, assorted bags, and spills of
gleaming coins.

Shee-it!

Slocum's blood began to reach the boiling point,
and he reached down at his side to caress the use-
polished grips of his Colt.

He shook his head and forced himself back to reality. That was a full score or more of Sioux braves over there a few yards away, and his first gunshot would send the whole pack of them howling on his trail. One six-shot cylinder of cartridges wasn't going to bother those boys. But, Lordy . . . !

Getting a grip on himself, Slocum forced his breathing to slow and his mind to clear.

His thoughts were racing furiously.

Luke Lowe had come here easily, without error, over a trail so faintly marked it would take an expert tracker—which Lowe certainly was not—to follow it the first time. Slocum had already been sure that Lowe had been over that trail before. He was equally sure the gambler had known about that campsite from the past, probably had used it before.

And now things were beginning to make sense.

It was no surprise at all that Lowe was a greedy, grasping cheat who thought first of himself—and of money immediately thereafter. Other people's problems were other people's problems to Lowe, especially when they might interfere with a profit that could be made.

Now the man was on the blanket with a pack of savages who were interested in just two things right now: killing the whites who were invading their sacred Black Hills and finding arms with which to do their killing.

Slocum could see no rifles and ammunition stacked up around the campfire, but he sure could see all that money.

And as two-plus-two most generally equals four, it seemed just as obvious and just as logical that Luke Lowe *must* be the white man John Slocum had so recently sworn to kill.

Shaking with anger, Slocum forced himself to

pay attention to what was going on in front of him. The social niceties apparently had been met by now, and the Sioux were about ready to get down to business, he thought.

None of them was wearing paint, of course. They were not here to fight but to bargain. And by now the ceremonial pipes had been around the circle all they were going to go. Now the fighting Sioux were beginning to drag out their own, smaller pipes of carved stone and to load them with their foul mixture—Slocum had tried it more than once in the past—of rank tobacco and kinnikinnic. It was nasty stuff, but it was also a clear signal that the preliminaries were over now.

Slocum made a careful exploration of the ground in front of him and bellied forward again as far as he dared while the Sioux were engaged in lighting up.

Lowe, for his part, seemed quite content and comfortable in his savage surroundings. He looked to be completely at ease, and Slocum wondered how much of that was real. The man was hardly a model of bravery. He must be sweating now beneath that calm exterior. Slocum hoped. Any small measure of discomfort for a man like that would be appreciated.

Bastard, Slocum thought. And no wonder he had wanted Slocum to stay in that camp back there. No wonder he had sicced Meg McGee onto Slocum's willing crotch. The man did not dare take a chance on not knowing where Slocum was while this meeting was in progress. If Slocum had gone on on his own earlier, it was too possible that he might run into the Sioux or see their tracks or spot the campfire from out on the surrounding prairie. Lowe knew he could not see the fire from the campsite. And he thought he knew equally

well that he could count on the lovely Meg to keep
Slocum's mind engaged with matters other than
Luke Lowe and his Sioux Indian friends.

It would have worked, too, Slocum realized, if
—like Lowe's cheating at the card table—he and
the woman had not been so damned obvious
about it all. With a little finesse, Lowe could have
been home free in this, too, and Slocum would
never have been the wiser for it.

"My people . . . suns . . . across the . . . great
. . . for all of time . . . power . . . kill . . ." One of
the Sioux was speaking English, and Slocum
strained his ears trying to catch the words.

Thank goodness for small favors, anyway. Apparently Lowe hadn't learned to speak the com-
plicated Dakota tongue. Neither had John Slocum.
But he was still just a little too far away. And he
had already moved forward as far as he dared.

Slocum swallowed. Damn these bastards one
and all and Luke Lowe twice over on top of that.
He wanted to *know*. He had already wriggled forward as far as was safe. So he would go a little
closer.

And if the murdering pricks caught him at his
spying, Luke Lowe was going to be the first to go
down. Slocum began to crawl forward.

"I understand," Lowe was telling them. "Yours
is a great people. A great people." He went on like
that at some length, and over his shoulder one of
the Sioux was translating his words into sign language for the others to follow.

Bless that greasy, louse-ridden Sioux prick, Slocum thought. The attention of the camp was on
the warrior's gracefully weaving hand talk. Slocum inched up a little closer still, although his
heart was beating so rapidly and so hard he found
it a source of wonder that the Sioux did not look

around to see where the tom-tom music was coming from.

"I understand your needs," Lowe was saying, "and I can fill those needs. I have the things your people need waiting for me at the place the whites call Bozeman. Already they have been shipped there, and there they await me, parked in grease inside the crates that are marked with other words so no one but you and I need know that the mighty Sioux Nation is to rise once again and regain their beloved Black Hills."

That information brought a chorus of excited grunts and bright smiles from the party gathered around the traitor.

Hell's green bells, Slocum thought. This particular crowd looked like it was already armed well enough to assault any fort the army had on the plains right now. Every damned warrior had a gun in his hand, and right now they were busy waving them in the air and shouting.

When they settled down again, Lowe went on with his sales pitch.

"But, my friends, before I can receive these rifles I must first pay for them. The crates were shipped in my name, but they cannot be claimed until I have paid. You know I do this as my favor to your great people, but the ways of the whites in St. Louis are strict, and they will not let me have the guns until I give them the money. Which I do not have. I am a friend of the great people, but I am a poor man. This is why I have asked for your help in this matter."

Shee-it. The bastard was already dripping money, and Slocum knew it. But he was going to get his up front from the Sioux. And Lowe knew it.

So, apparently, did the Sioux. They seemed to accept this as a normal routine of business.

"This you told us before," the Sioux spokesman said in a solemn voice. "You have been straight with us, Lefarge."

Jesus, Slocum thought. Luke Lowe was about as French as your average Dutchman, but he was good at covering his tracks. If any sassy blueleg from one of those army posts should get wind of the arms sales going on up in this neck of the woods, the army would go tearing off in search of some Frenchman. And they might find some poor bastard to hang it on, too, but it wouldn't be ol' Luke Lowe if they ever did. Lowe was about as slimy as they came, Slocum figured.

It was going to be a real pleasure to discuss this when there weren't a bunch of Sioux around to protect the man.

"We have done as you asked," the Indian went on. "Here is what we have brought you." He spread his hands and pointed to the piles of money on the blanket between Lowe and the fire.

"It is good," Lowe said.

Slocum thought he could see the greed flashing in Lowe's eyes now as he was able to openly survey the impressive amount of cash that was being offered to him.

"There is little value on the blanket," Lowe lied, "but perhaps it will be enough. For some if not for all. I must count it to know, and you know that the white man's scales in the place called Bozeman are not always straight. They would cheat me as they would cheat you. But I will do what I can to help the great Sioux people. If necessary I will put in from my own pocket all that I have in order to help the Sioux people."

Stupid shit, Slocum was thinking. All Lowe had going for him was greed. As a con man the fellow was a bust. He hadn't even bothered to find out that Sioux was a word used by the whites to identify this tribe. They called themselves Dakota or Lakota or sometimes Nakota. They probably understood the difference; Slocum didn't. But at least he wasn't dumb enough to think they were Sioux in their own camps. Lowe either didn't know or didn't care, and the Sioux were too polite to correct him, apparently. And too eager. This guy was supposed to be their ticket to living happily ever after in the sacred Black Hills, after all.

"You are a good friend," the Sioux spokesman said. He made a sign, and several of the younger warriors stepped forward to begin wrapping the gold and currency and coins into the blanket the money had been lying on.

"The yellow dirt that the whites value is heavy," the Indian said. "We will place it on a pony for you." He smiled. "The pony is a gift for our great friend Lefarge."

Lowe went into a fit of effusive thanks for the gift they had given him. From the way he went on, the pony was a hell of a lot more valuable than any old packload of gold.

Yet even from where he lay in the cover of darkness, Slocum could see that there must have been —who could know?—$10,000? $20,000? It was an awful lot, he knew that. An awful lot. Enough that it took a packhorse to tote it all.

And Lowe was telling them he was going to have to dig into his own kick to buy them a few rifles. Slocum wondered just how many guns Lowe was expected to deliver for that huge pile of treasure.

Shee-it!

Slocum had already seen far more than he had ever expected to see, and some of the younger warriors looked like they were getting restless. It would only take one of them slipping away from the fire to take a piss for Slocum to get himself discovered. Which he did not think would end up in a particularly comfortable fashion.

It was time to get the hell out of there, he decided.

Even more cautiously than he had crawled forward, he began now to back away.

His thoughts as he moved could have served as an advance course in creative cussing.

31

"Where is Meg?" Lowe asked as he strolled into the camp.

Slocum was lying on the ground, lounging against the cracked leather seat of the saddle Lowe had found for him in Deadwood. He was smoking a cigar, and he grinned at Lowe. To himself he said, yes, come into the camp. Come and smoke with me. You're good at smoking during council. Do this with your executioner too, little man. Though in his camp there is no fire to warm your bones before you die.

Slocum almost laughed. There was no fire, no hot food here, because of Slocum's cautious insistence. No wonder Lowe had been so free about the idea of lighting a fire in hostile country. After all, the Sioux knew he would be there. They were expecting him to meet them.

"She went off to take a leak," Slocum answered. "A very modest lady, you know."

Lowe grunted and hunkered down next to his blankets. There was no sign of the packhorse carrying his treasure, Slocum saw. Not that he expected the gambler to bring the pony into camp with him. That would have raised questions, and as far as Lowe knew, he was still getting away with his deception.

"Would you like a cigar?"

"What?" Lowe asked.

"I said, would you like a cigar?" Slocum uncoiled his tall, hard frame from the ground and took the few strides required to reach Luke Lowe's side.

He towered over the gambler as he removed a cheap cigar from his breast pocket and, with the long, wickedly heavy Bowie that never left his belt, carefully trimmed the twist from the tip of the stogie.

"Here." Slocum leaned down and inserted the clipped end of the cigar between Lowe's teeth. With his left hand—the right continued to balance the Bowie—he pulled a match from his pocket and dragged it alight across his belt buckle.

"I don't want the damn thing," Lowe said. He removed the cigar from his mouth and gave Slocum a look that was filled with curiosity—but not yet with fear. "What's gotten into you?" he demanded.

"Smoke your cigar, Lowe," Slocum said quietly.

"I told you . . ."

"And I told you. Smoke the fucking cigar. Or I'll feed it to you." Slocum was riding on the thin edge of control now. Hatred crackled in his voice, and Lowe could not possibly have missed hearing it there.

"What the *hell* is wrong with you?" Lowe asked. But he returned the cigar to his mouth and accepted the light Slocum offered him.

"That's better," Slocum said with satisfaction. He was more in control of himself now. He wanted to take his time.

Slocum stood looming over the gambler, watching him with the intensity of an eagle circling above an unsuspecting rabbit a thousand feet below. "Smoke it on down, Luke. Get a good coal going there."

"I don't understand this," Lowe complained.

"You will."

Lowe craned his neck from side to side, trying to look past Slocum into the deep shadows unrelieved here by firelight. "How long has Meg been gone. Maybe I should go look for her."

"She's just fine, Luke. Just fine."

"But maybe . . ." The gambler started to rise. Slocum's left fist crashed down against his shoulder, sending him sprawling into the dirt on his ass. "What the fuck was that for?" The man was angry now. But still not yet frightened.

That was reasonable, Slocum thought. The miserable son of a bitch was still too elated over his profits from the Sioux to be thinking in terms of his own death.

"Don't leave, Luke. Not just yet. We have some talking to do, you and me."

"Talking? I don't understand. I just want to find Meg and see that she's all ri . . ."

Slocum kicked him in the gut. Hard.

"I said, we're going to talk, Luke. Pay attention to me." Slocum's voice was ice in the air between them. He was as calm as death now.

Lowe curled into a pain-filled ball on the ground at Slocum's feet. He cried out in the silence that surrounded them.

"Sit up, Luke. We're fixing to have that talk now."

"But I . . ." Slocum's boot lashed out again, sinking with the sound of a butcher's tenderizing spiked hammer striking beefsteak, sinking deep into the vee between the gambler's legs.

This time the cry was a howling shriek of agony, and the gambler rolled and twisted on the ground.

Good boy, Slocum thought. That war cry would do your friends proud.

Lowe was gasping for air and his face was drained of all color. He began to crawl on his hands and knees, weakly trying now to evade this madman that he could not begin to understand. "What . . . ?"

"I said you should sit up, Luke. Talk to me." Slocum was in front of him again, had moved with him. His feeble efforts at crawling brought him to John Slocum's booted feet. Lowe looked up with a dawning terror in his eyes. The man's face twisted, and he looked as if he were about to weep.

"What have I *done?*" Lowe wailed.

"I told you, Luke. We're going to talk. You and me."

"But what have I . . . ?"

"Don't worry about it. Not now," Slocum said. "You won't have to worry about anything. Not ever again." He was grinning now. That terrible, terrifying grin that spoke of death and long rotted corpses and the green fire of hatred and combat. Lowe dropped his eyes away from the sight of John Slocum's face. He could not stand to look into those eyes a moment longer.

"But I don't . . ."

"Of course you do, Luke. You know. But first I want you to tell me something, if you please."

"Wha . . . ?"

"The pony, Luke. The packhorse with all the goodies on it. Where did you tie it?" Slocum's grin became all the broader. "We wouldn't want the poor brute to thirst to death or anything. After all, Luke, we're civilized men. We aren't savages. We have feelings for poor, dumb beasts, don't we."

Lowe's face was a complete mask of terror now. "How did you . . . ?"

"I'm a sneaky sonuvabitch, Luke. Can't hardly be trusted to stay where people want me to be. I thought you knew that." Slocum was almost laughing now. His casual attitude made the moment all the more terrible for Lowe. As Slocum intended it should. "Come now, Luke. Tell me. Then we can get on with the rest of our conversation."

A flicker of defiance showed in the greedy gambler's eyes. This was the one deterrent he might still possess. Slocum wanted to find the pony. Lowe would not tell him. It might be enough to keep him alive. It might . . .

Summoning all of his reserves of strength and purpose, trying his weak best to contain the pain that was wracking his guts, Lowe began to pull himself erect.

He clutched Slocum's pantlegs and used his enemy's legs as a prop to support himself while he climbed painfully to his knees and, after a struggle, to his feet. For the first time, he stood facing Slocum.

"We could . . ." A dart of pain lanced through him as he tried to straighten his back, and for a moment he was breathless and ashen-faced. He struggled. He managed it. He looked John Slocum in the eyes, desperately trying to pretend that he did not see death reflected there. "We could make a deal, John . . . a deal. Just between us. You and me. There's lots . . . lots of money. You know that. Enough for both of us."

Slocum grinned at him. "There's enough for me, I'll grant you that, Luke."

"A deal, Slocum. You and me. Lots of money. More where that came from. Plenty."

Slocum laughed. "Yeah, Luke, there's lots of money to be found. In every pocket of every white man who travels the roads into the Black Hills or out again. That's true."

Lowe shook his head. "You don't know that. *I* don't know that. We don't *have* to know where it comes from. That isn't our affair, is it? We don't *know.*"

"I know," Slocum said softly. His voice was like a caress in the night air. "I know, Luke."

"But you . . ."

"In your pack, Luke. On that pony you don't want to tell me about. Wrapped up in that blanket and put there by those two tall bucks. You remember them. One of them in a blue army field blouse an' the other in a breechclout with red beading down both sides. You do remember those boys, don't you?"

Lowe's eyes were popping wide. There was no possible way anyone but himself could know this. No way at all.

"Yeah, I see that you do remember them, Luke. That's good. You're doing real good now, Luke." Slocum smiled and reached out to gently pat Lowe on the shoulder.

"Well, in that pack, Luke. The one we both remember. There's a lady's purse in that pack. Do you want me to tell you how much money is in that purse? I can, you know. I know that purse. I know how much Jennifer Porter had in it when she left Deadwood the other morning. And, Luke" —his voice was even softer now, chillingly gentle—"I saw Miss Porter's body when your friends were finished with her. That was a nice lady, Luke. A friend of mine. I liked her."

Lowe began to squeeze his eyes shut, as if blocking the sight could somehow alter the fact.

Slocum reached forward again and gently patted Luke Lowe's trembling shoulder.

"You'll feel better soon, Luke. You'll feel a lot better real soon."

The gambler had to know he was a dead man now. He had nothing to deal with at all. Slocum did not really care about the pack animal. The tall, lethal outlaw would find it on his own easily enough. And even if he did not, he would kill Luke Lowe regardless.

But as afraid as he was, Lowe was not going to stand and wait to die.

The gambler stretched his arm down at his side and arched his wrist inward, springing the spring-steel clip buckled to the inside of his forearm. A .41-caliber percussion derringer slid into place in his soft, deft fingers, which were so expert at the manipulation of playing cards.

He tried not to look at Slocum. Tried to give his enemy no indication of what was to come. Stealthily he began to raise his hand.

"I wondered when you'd get around to that, Luke."

Lowe looked up. Looked into John Slocum's laughing, evil eyes. He thought he could see traces of green fire flashing there.

Slocum's right hand flashed instead, and the massive Bowie arced through the space between them.

Lowe felt a blow against the back of his hand and, dumbfounded, looked down.

The derringer was no longer there.

Oh, Jesus! His *fingers* were no longer there. His hand ended in a ragged, dripping row of stumps just past the knuckles.

Luke Lowe screamed.

"Worried about your future, Luke?" Slocum asked calmly. "Don't be. You don't have one."

The Bowie flashed again, and the right side of Lowe's chest ran red with blood. A tiny holster containing another hideout gun fell to the ground at Lowe's feet.

Lowe's shrieks caught in his throat this time. He was beyond agony now.

Or so he thought.

"This is going to take a while, Luke. The dying, that is."

Slocum slid the thick, razor-honed blade of the Bowie forward. The big blade went in just above Lowe's belt buckle. Slocum stood with the knife lodged in the flesh of the gambler. He smiled. "You'll be glad when it finally does happen, Luke. I can promise you that."

With the grin still on his lean, brown face, John Slocum twisted his wrist and the sharp blade turned. Lowe screamed.

"You're getting better at it, Luke. Your friends would be proud of you."

Slocum stepped back and turned away.

Abner Kraus and Jennifer Porter had their revenge now.

32

Slocum swung onto the grulla horse and checked to see that the lead ropes were secure. He did not want to lose the scruffy spotted pony with the blanket lashed to its back. The carpetbags were tied onto the saddle of the horse that had been Luke Lowe's.

"Are you ready?" he asked.

Meg McGee gave him a look that was half anger, half fear. "Do I have any choice?"

"You might as well quit bitching," he told her. "I was nice enough to untie you. You might show a little appreciation."

The woman mouthed an extremely vulgar word.

"Not bad," Slocum said judiciously. "With a little effort you can do better, though."

Meg glared at him. She stood beside her horse for a moment, and when Slocum made no offer to dismount and help her into her saddle she stepped lightly aboard without assistance. "You are a prick, John Slocum," she said.

"Yes, ma'am. There's lots of folks that agree with you." He glanced over his shoulder to assure himself once again that the pack pony was all right. He did not want to lose it. He shook his head.

Such a lot of money. He had no idea how much,

really. There was something over $2,100 in currency and coins alone. And that was without even beginning to count the gold dust that would make up the great bulk of the value. For that he would need a set of scales, but he knew the amount had to be many times the value of the cash. Most of what came out of Deadwood was, after all, in raw gold sifted out of the dirt and the flowing streams by men who were now dead. And by women, in their own way.

Slocum felt no compunctions about the way Luke Lowe must have died. None whatsoever.

He had found the packhorse with no trouble at all. Untied Meg McGee and moved their camp the night before, leaving Lowe to die alone in his agony on the ground around on the other side of the long, abruptly rising hill where the Sioux had held their meeting.

Now all Slocum had to do was to keep an eye out for those Sioux and get the hell away from this part of the country. With Lowe's money, that is. He grinned. This wasn't turning out so bad after all.

He looked around toward the woman. She was seated on her sidesaddle but was shifting around with a look of annoyed discomfort on her pretty face.

"John," she said.

"Mmmm?"

"There really are cases of carbines and ammunition waiting in Bozeman, you know."

"I couldn't claim that I'm amazed by that."

"Because of Luke?" She laughed. "You should be. Do you remember when we first met? Back during that attack on the stagecoach?"

"I ain't real likely to forget it this quick, lady."

"Those poor braves weren't attacking us by accident," Meg said. "They were after Luke in particular. He had taken their money for a shipment of rifles, then got a better offer from another band. That's why they were after him."

Slocum shook his head. He really should not be surprised any longer by the venality of Luke Lowe.

"I don't think you get my point," Meg said.

"You had one?"

She smiled. "Of course, darling. I was just thinking that, well, you and I . . . we might adopt a good idea when we find one, dear."

"I think you're right, Meg. I think I'm definitely missing your point."

"What I mean, John dear, is that those crates are waiting for us in Bozeman. And we do already have the money this band up here collected. We could pick up the carbines and go make amends with that band to the south. I'm sure they would have more money by now, dear." She smiled brightly. "We are so *very* good together, John. I'm sure we would get along just famously as partners."

"Dear Meg. Sweet Meg. Great-fuck Meg. If you mention that idea to me again, lovely Meg, I personally will slit your pretty throat and watch while your pretty tits get all red and sticky. You wouldn't want that now, would you?"

He meant it, too.

"It was only a suggestion, dear."

"Yeah. Right." He shook his head wearily. "Are you finally ready?"

"In a minute. This damn saddle . . . or maybe my petticoats are just bunching up under here. Wait a minute."

She dropped lithely to the ground and reached beneath her skirt to rearrange her undergarments.

Son of a bitch.

When she pulled her hand out she had a ducky little bulldog revolver filling it. Small and short but pure hell for power. The slug it threw was every bit as big as the one that Slocum's heavy Colt spit.

"I didn't want to do this, dear. But what can a girl do?"

"Where'd you get that thing?"

"Oh, I really don't like to go unprepared, John."

Come to think of it, he realized, she had always shucked her clothing more or less all at once. She had never given him a good look at the petticoats that were under her dresses. She probably had a holster or clip of some sort built into the damn things.

Slocum felt like something of a fool.

"Do be a good fellow now and let loose of that lead rope, dear," she said.

Unlike her recently departed benefactor, Meg McGee looked to be damned well competent with a short gun. She handled the bulldog like she jolly well knew what she was doing.

"That's a love," she said. "Now ride over there just a little ways. That's right."

She mounted her horse without ever once allowing the .45 revolver to leave its point of aim dead center on Slocum's belly. With one hand holding the gun and the other guiding her horse, she moved up to the spotted pony and picked up the lead rope, tying the animal to her own saddle by the knee crook that jutted like a drunken roping horn from the fancy sidesaddle.

"Very good, dear."

"Are you sure you really want to do this?"

"I am positive. Don't be a bore now, John. I wouldn't like that."

"I think you're making a mistake, Meg. There

are Indians out here, you know. And they wouldn't even dream of making a business deal with a woman. If they get a look at you, you're dead, lady. Thoroughly raped first, of course, but soon enough dead."

"Pooh. You forget, dear, I have access to the guns they want. They won't harm a hair on my head."

"I'm trying to tell you, Meg. Sioux warriors are the same as a businessman in Sioux City. Them boys don't think women are hardly people. Especially white women. They won't give you a chance to make their dreams come true. They'll just drop their breechclouts and have at you, and when they're done there won't hardly be enough left to identify you as a woman, much less as Meg McGee."

"You're trying to frighten me, John. That is very rude of you. Useless, too. Now get off your horse, please, and turn him loose. Yes. That's nice, dear. Thank you."

"What do you think you're doing, you idiot bitch?"

"I'm leaving you here, of course." She smiled. "I suppose I really should kill you. Luke certainly would have. But I'm not ungenerous. And you are quite a lovely fuck. It would be a shame to take a pole like that out of existence, wouldn't it?" She blew him a kiss. "Eventually I'm sure you will be able to walk that horse down. By then I shall be long gone. And for safety's sake, I think I will go up there where the Indians are. They won't hurt me, and they will do very nicely to discourage you from trying to follow me."

"Dammit, Meg, you're fixing to commit suicide if you ride up that hill. Hell, those boys will have their paint on by now. They'll be keeping an eye on everything that moves down here on the grass. They might already have spotted us, for Christ's sake. We need to get out of here. Now. The both of us."

"It was a nice try, dear, but I don't really believe you want to share all this lovely money with me. And do remember, I am the one who knows the labels those arms crates bear. I can get them without you, but you can't get them without me, dear." She smiled. "Ta-ta, love. Have a nice day."

Without a hint of any apparent fear, the stupid bitch gigged her horse and rode it, with the spotted pony trailing decidedly behind, up the hillside toward the Sioux camp.

Jesus, Slocum thought.

But that damned bulldog revolver was aimed his way every step she took until it was too late for him to try to stop her.

He felt sorry for her, somehow. Poor, stupid damned female.

With a sigh of regret—more for the treasure that was loaded onto the spotted pony than for the ignorant woman who held its lead rope—Slocum began to try to walk up to the spooky grulla that did not yet know him well enough to stand while he approached.

Some time before he finally caught the animal Slocum thought he heard distant whooping and jeering and the beat of savage drums.

No, he thought, he was not going up that hillside after her. Not now especially.

He managed to catch up to the grulla and swung aboard it. He still had his Colt and his rifle. And—he touched the heavy roll beneath his shirt—the money belt and wallet Luke Lowe had been carrying on his person. Slocum hadn't counted the take there, but it was better than having his hair lifted. John Slocum was no coward, but he wasn't a fucking idiot either.

He reined the grulla toward Bozeman and began getting the hell out of there while he still could.